Drug Abuse

Look for these and other books in the Lucent
Overview series:

Abortion	The Holocaust
Acid Rain	Homeless Children
AIDS	Illegal Immigration
Alcoholism	Illiteracy
Animal Rights	Immigration
Artificial Organs	Mental Illness
The Beginning of Writing	Money
The Brain	Ocean Pollution
Cancer	Oil Spills
Censorship	The Olympic Games
Child Abuse	Organ Transplants
Cities	Ozone
The Collapse of the Soviet Union	Pesticides
Dealing with Death	Police Brutality
Death Penalty	Population
Democracy	Prisons
Drug Abuse	Rainforests
Drugs and Sports	Recycling
Drug Trafficking	The Reunification of Germany
Eating Disorders	Schools
Endangered Species	Smoking
The End of Apartheid in South Africa	Space Exploration
Energy Alternatives	Special Effects in the Movies
Espionage	Teen Alcoholism
Euthanasia	Teen Pregnancy
Extraterrestrial Life	Teen Suicide
Family Violence	The UFO Challenge
Gangs	The United Nations
Garbage	The U.S. Congress
Gay Rights	The U.S. Presidency
The Greenhouse Effect	Vanishing Wetlands
Gun Control	Vietnam
Hate Groups	World Hunger
Hazardous Waste	Zoos

Drug Abuse

by Carolyn Kott Washburne

LUCENT
BOOKS

LUCENT Overview Series

Library of Congress Cataloging-in-Publication Data

Washburne, Carolyn Kott.
    Drug abuse / by Carolyn Kott Washburne.
       p. cm. — (Lucent overview series)
    Includes bibliographical references and index.
    Summary: An overview of the problem of drug abuse and efforts
to combat it.
    ISBN 1-56006-169-3 (lib ed : alk. paper)
    1. Drug abuse—Juvenile literature. 2. Drugs—Juvenile
literature. [1. Drug abuse. 2. Drugs.] I. Title. II. Series.
HV5809.5.W37   1996
362.29—dc20
                                    95-16200
                                          CIP
                                           AC

© Copyright 1996 by Lucent Books, Inc.
P.O. Box 289011, San Diego, CA 92198-9011
Printed in the U.S.A.

Contents

Introduction

IN LOS ANGELES a twenty-something fashion photographer goes to the Room, a back-alley bar with no sign over its entrance. Around midnight a man walks in and hands the photographer a packet of heroin in exchange for a hundred dollars. The photographer disappears into the men's room and emerges a few minutes later, grinning and obviously high.

In a central city neighborhood of Chicago the latest cheap high for teenagers is a blunt, also known as a marijuana cigar. To make a blunt, the teens open a cigar and mix the tobacco with marijuana. If they can get their hands on other drugs, they mix them in, too. Sometimes they dip the cigar in malt liquor, creating what is called a B-40.

In New York City a top Wall Street economist takes a four-week medical leave of absence from his firm to enter a drug rehabilitation program. He has almost ruined his career with cocaine and alcohol abuse. He says the pressure of his job was in part to blame. "You think you're a superman, you think you can do anything," he says. "I felt invincible and that there were no limits as to how late I could stay up or how much I could travel."

The photographer, the teens, and the economist are all among the estimated six million Americans who have a serious drug problem. Most of these people go to school, hold jobs, raise families, and

(Opposite page) An addict injects cocaine into his arm at a crack house in New York's South Bronx. Cocaine is the drug of choice for three-quarters of the approximately two million hardcore drug users in the United States.

7

appear to be leading normal lives. But they actually lead double lives—dangerous double lives.

According to the federal government's Office of National Drug Control Policy, about two million of these people are considered hard-core addicts who consume most of the illegal drugs in the United States. About three-quarters of them are hooked on cocaine and about one-quarter on heroin. Many of them are also alcoholics. These hard-core users commit a high percentage of property crimes, fill up the nation's jails, and burden the health care system. While drug use and abuse can occur in all social and economic classes, hard-core addicts are more often poor people, many of whom are minorities.

In addition to the six million Americans with a serious drug problem, there are an estimated three and a half million people who use drugs occasionally—at least once in the previous year but less often than every month. Occasional drug use has actually dropped since 1988, when an estimated five and a half million American adults fell into that category.

This drop in casual use is about the only positive sign in the otherwise bleak story of drug use in the United States. This story is especially bleak as it concerns young people. In the late 1970s drug use by young people in the United States reached a peak and then began to decline. Experts credit this decline to the vigorous drug education campaigns that were conducted nationwide by concerned parents, teachers, and elected officials.

Beginning in 1993, however, drug use among young people—from eighth graders through high school seniors—began to rise and has continued to rise. This is according to a yearly study conducted by the University of Michigan Institute for Social Research. The drugs used most often are stimulants, LSD, inhalants, and marijuana.

Drug abusers come from all walks of life. Most hold jobs and lead what appear to be normal lives.

U.S. marshals raid a Washington, D.C., crack house in 1989. Law enforcement stepped up its antidrug efforts between 1988 and 1993 as part of the Bush administration's war on drugs.

Regardless of whether the rates of drug use are increasing or declining, the United States has a serious drug problem. Fighting this problem has been a priority of the federal government for more than twenty years. In 1988 President George Bush declared his well-known war on drugs. From 1988 to 1993 the government spent $52 billion to fight drug abuse. The goals of the war were to slow the production of illegal drugs overseas and within the United States, stop the flow of drugs into the country, and reduce the demand for them by drug users.

Yet by 1994 by all accounts, including those of the federal government, worldwide production of drugs was up. Worse, illegal drugs available in the United States were easier to get than ever before. Many federal, local, and state officials—as well as hundreds of thousands of citizens—feel frustrated and confused about what to do.

The problem of drug abuse is a vexing one. To understand why the best minds in the country have not been able to solve it requires understanding some complex issues: what drug abuse is, who abuses drugs, and the harmful effects that drugs have on individuals and communities. Understanding these issues is an important first step in solving the problem.

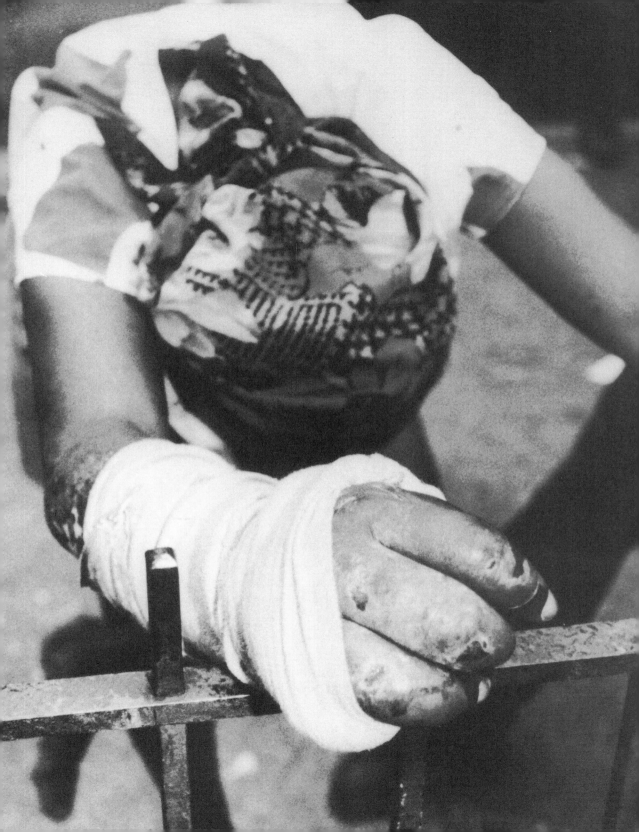

1

What Is Drug Abuse?

WILLIAM WAS LIVING the good life. He had a beautiful family, a big house in the suburbs, everything he had ever wanted. Then he started sniffing cocaine and almost lost it all. "It's a lie that cocaine's not addictive," he says. "I didn't choose to be an addict. Quitting cocaine was the only thing I couldn't do by myself. I'll be a recovering addict day by day for the rest of my life."

Drugs: powerful substances

William experienced firsthand the awesome power of drugs. A drug is a chemical that acts on the brain and nervous system. It can cause changes in feelings, behavior, and the way the body works. A drug can be as old as opium—discovered between 4000 and 2000 B.C.—or as new as a designer drug manufactured last week in an illegal laboratory. For the most part, drugs are beneficial. It is difficult to think of what modern life would be like without prescription and over-the-counter drugs.

But any drug can become dangerous if used unwisely or abused. Drug abuse means using a drug in such a way that it begins to have harmful effects on the mind and body. This could mean

(Opposite page) A woman waits to be searched by Washington, D.C., police during a drug raid. Her arm is swollen and infected as a result of injecting drugs with dirty needles.

11

taking too much of the drug or taking more than one drug at a time without a doctor's supervision. Relying on a drug to have a good time or just to get through the day is called dependence. Dependence turns into addiction when a person is unable to stop using the drug.

Some drugs are physically addictive, others are psychologically addictive. Physical addiction occurs when a person uses a drug over time. Amphetamines, drugs that speed up the nervous system, are one type of physically addictive drug.

Deborah, for example, became physically addicted to the pain medication she took after a car accident. At first she denied her addiction. She excused it because she was having bad back and knee pain. When her doctors refused to prescribe the pills anymore, she began stealing prescription pads and writing her own prescriptions. "My choice of drug was Percocet, but if I could get other pain pills, like codeine, Darvocet, Talwin, I

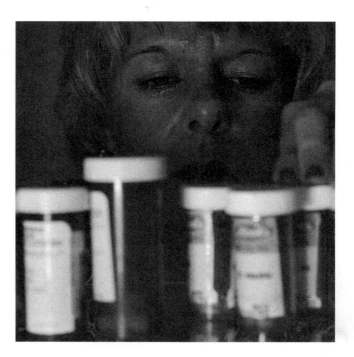

While drug abuse is usually associated with illegal drugs like cocaine and heroin, legally prescribed drugs can also lead to addiction.

did," she says. Eventually Deborah got caught and spent a year in a federal prison for forging prescriptions.

Other drugs are psychologically addictive. This means that people feel they cannot do without them. Over-the-counter sleeping pills, for example, are usually not strong enough to put someone to sleep. Yet many people say they simply cannot fall asleep without their pills.

With either physical or psychological addiction, the drug often becomes part of the body's chemistry, so that the person cannot feel well without it. The person usually builds up tolerance, which means that increasing amounts of the drug must be taken to get the same effect. Stopping use of the drug can cause painful physical symptoms, which is called withdrawal. And taking more of the drug than the body can handle may lead to an overdose. Overdoses can cause physical problems, such as brain or heart damage, and even death.

The four stages of drug abuse

It is sometimes difficult to tell when a person is abusing drugs, especially if the abuse is in its beginning stages. Also, the symptoms of drug use and abuse—that is, how the person looks and talks and acts—are different for different drugs. Even so, the Office for Substance Abuse Prevention of the U.S. Public Health Service has classified four basic stages of drug use.

Stage One is beginning or casual use, often in social situations such as parties. In Stage One there may be no obvious changes in behavior. This does not mean, however, that drug abuse has not begun to take hold. Many young people and some adults believe that using a drug once or twice is safe. However, because young bodies are particularly susceptible to drugs and their effects, no mind-altering drug can be used safely by a young person. And some adults are more at risk than others of becoming addicted because of physical, emotional, and genetic characteristics.

Stage Two involves more frequent use of drugs as the person actively seeks to get high—that is, to feel the exciting, pleasurable, mind-altering effects of the drug. At this point the user usually establishes a reliable source for obtaining drugs and may add midweek use of drugs to previous habits of weekend use at parties. Among adolescents, significant clues may be changes in friends, deterioration of school performance, and possibly a general lack of motivation.

In Stage Three all the person can think about is getting high. Daily use of drugs, depression, and thoughts of suicide are common. Family tensions increase, and the person may be stopped or arrested for drunken driving or encounter some other trouble with the law.

In Stage Four the person needs more and more of the drug just to feel okay. Physical signs such as coughing, frequent sore throats, weight loss, tiredness, and irritability are now common. Blackouts—periods when the drug user cannot remember what happened—can also occur. Family life is usually very tense, and the person may resort to crime to obtain money to buy drugs.

Legal drugs

Legal drugs are those that have been approved for sale to the public. This can be obtained either with a prescription from a doctor or over the counter—that is, without a prescription—at a drugstore or grocery store. A common type of prescription drug is an antibiotic, such as penicillin. There are hundreds of over-the-counter drugs, from aspirin to first-aid lotions, from cold remedies to creams that help heal sports injuries.

Alcohol and tobacco are also legal drugs when bought by an adult.

Tranquilizers

Tranquilizers, originally developed in the 1930s, act on the body's central nervous and autonomic nervous systems, two of the main systems that allow the human body to function. The central nervous system, which consists of the brain and spinal cord, coordinates the activity of the entire nervous system by receiving sensory impulses and transmitting motor impulses. The autonomic nervous system governs involuntary actions of the intestines, heart, and glands, such as the secretion of fluids. There are two types of tranquilizers, whose street, or slang, names are

Crack cocaine users can quickly reach Stage Four of drug use— the stage in which a person needs progressively more of the drug just to feel okay.

downers or "tranks": antianxiety and antipsychotic. Antianxiety tranquilizers relax muscles, relieve tension, and help people cope with emotional crises. These tranquilizers are often used in conjunction with psychotherapy. The world's most commonly prescribed drug, diazepam—the generic form of Valium—is an antianxiety tranquilizer. Antipsychotic tranquilizers are prescribed primarily for people with serious mental illness, such as psychosis and schizophrenia.

Small amounts of tranquilizers can produce calmness and relaxed muscles; larger doses can cause slurred speech, staggering, and altered perceptions. Very large doses can interfere with breathing, which can lead to coma and even death.

Most tranquilizers have not become popular street drugs. Street drugs are those that are either illegal altogether or prescription drugs that are used illegally. Tranquilizers do not produce a pleasurable high; they tend to cause confusion, depression, and visual disturbances, among other side effects. Diazepam is the exception because its effects are milder than other tranquilizers—most users experience pleasant feelings of euphoria, or elation, while taking diazepam. And because it is so widely prescribed, it is relatively easy to obtain illegally.

Barbiturates

Barbiturates, also called "barbs," are derived from barbituric acid and are used as sedatives, that is, to calm nervousness or excitement. Although over twenty-five hundred different types have been produced, only about fifty have been approved for medical use, and only about ten are prescribed regularly. Some of the best-known barbiturates are phenobarbital (Nembutal, "phennies"), amobarbital (Amytal), secobarbital (Seconal, reds, red devils), pentobarbital (yellow jackets), and secobarbital-amobarbital combinations (Tuinal, rainbows, "tooies").

Doctors prescribe barbiturates to treat tension, anxiety, sleeplessness, high blood pressure, and illnesses that cause seizures, such as epilepsy. The short-term effects of barbiturates are similar to those of an alcoholic high. The person may at first feel relaxed then experience slurred speech, staggering, slowed reactions, and poor memory. Long-term effects include increased tolerance and serious dependency. In fact, some professionals feel that barbiturate dependency is the most dangerous of all the chemical dependencies because it is so difficult to overcome. The most common form of death by overdosing is using barbiturates and alcohol together—either on purpose or accidentally.

Narcotics

Narcotics, also called opiates, have powerful painkilling and sedative effects. They are made from opium, the dried juice of the unripe seedpod of the opium poppy. Historians believe that opium was discovered in the area of the Mediterranean Sea somewhere between 4000 and 2000 B.C. By 400 B.C. Greek doctors had developed medical uses for it.

A Turkish woman collects the seeds of opium poppy plants. The dried juice of these seeds is used to make narcotics like morphine and heroin.

Narcotics include opium, morphine, heroin, and codeine. Synthetic narcotics have also been developed. These include methadone, which is also used to treat heroin dependence, meperidine (Demerol), and oxycodone (Percodan). In low doses narcotics block the sensation of pain without interfering greatly with the central nervous system. This means that they are effective pain-killers. In higher doses, however, users become very drowsy and can fall into a stupor or coma. Over time tolerance develops, to the point where a heavy user can tolerate several times the dose that would kill someone who had not built up tolerance.

Amphetamines

Amphetamines (speed, uppers) are powerful stimulants that act on the central nervous system. They are used by millions of people both legally and illegally, such as in the form of diet pills or stay-awake pills for studying. Some of the most common amphetamines are dextroamphetamine ("dexies," "dex"), benzamphetamine (bennies), methamphetamine ("meth," crystal, ice), and biphetamine (black Cadillacs).

Amphetamines can be obtained by prescription, but since 1970 laws have been passed to limit production of amphetamines. Most doctors are now wary of prescribing them because the potential for abuse is so high. Today most amphetamines available on the street are manufactured in illegal laboratories.

Amphetamines, at least in the short term, literally speed people up. Users feel as though they have more energy, can stay awake longer, and can concentrate better. This is probably true at lower doses, because the heart and breathing rates do increase. But extended use or high doses can lead to blurred vision, dizziness, sleeplessness, irregular heartbeat, and even a stroke or heart failure. In addition to the physical effects, users can feel restless, anxious, and moody; over time they may even develop hallucinations and paranoia.

Steroids

Anabolic steroids, developed in the 1930s, are a group of compounds similar to the male sex hormone, testosterone. There are a few legitimate medical uses for steroids, such as to treat severe burns, anemia, and some forms of cancer. However, steroids are seldom prescribed today by reputable physicians.

Less than reputable physicians, however, prescribe steroids to improve the performance of high school, college, and professional athletes. Steroids, when combined with a program of exercise and diet, may help increase body weight and muscle strength. But people who use steroids are risking more than seventy side effects. The physical effects range from sterility to cancer. The psychological effects include depression and aggression, which is known as "roid rage."

Perhaps the best-known victim of steroid abuse was professional football player Lyle Alzado of the Oakland Raiders, who died of brain cancer in 1992. Alzado said publicly that he believed his years of steroid use had caused or at least contributed to the cancer. The signs of steroid use, along with quick weight gain and muscle development, include trembling, purple or red spots on the body, and unpleasant breath odor.

Inhalants

Inhalants are chemicals—usually gases or liquids—that cause intoxication when inhaled in sufficient quantities. Common household products—an estimated fourteen hundred are sold over the counter—are used by young people

Professional football player Lyle Alzado spoke out about the dangers of steroids after being diagnosed with terminal brain cancer. He believed steroid use may have caused his cancer.

because the sniffers, or inhalants, are legal, easy to obtain, and cheap. Using these substances to get high is called sniffing or huffing.

One type of inhalant is volatile solvents. These include paint thinner, lighter fluid, fingernail polish remover, cleaning fluid, plastic cement, and gasoline. Sniffing these causes a temporary high. At the same time, it depresses the central nervous system, lowers heart and breathing rates, and impairs judgment and muscle coordination. Another type of inhalant is aerosol propellant gases, such as fluorocarbons, including Freon. Some of these are harmless, but others are deadly. This is because a gas under pressure is extremely cold when it is released from the container; it can freeze the throat or lungs when sniffed.

Other commonly abused inhalants include nitrous oxide (laughing gas), which is used for dental work, and amyl and butyl nitrite (poppers, snappers), which are prescribed for heart problems and asthma.

Illegal drugs

Illegal drugs are those that are against the law to make, sell, buy, or possess. These drugs include marijuana, cocaine, heroin, and PCP. It is also against the law to illegally obtain and use a legal drug, such as by stealing or forging a prescription, using someone else's prescription, or accumulating prescriptions from several doctors at one time.

Marijuana

Marijuana is a plant in the cannabis family; other common types of cannabis are hashish (hash) and THC (tetrahydrocannabinol). Street names for marijuana are pot, reefer, weed, dope, grass, ganja, Mary Jane, and sinsemilla. Marijuana, which is usually smoked, produces both

Pictured is a baggie of marijuana and assorted paraphernalia. A popular drug with young people, marijuana can decrease a person's ability and motivation to learn.

relaxation and a state of heightened awareness. Some people believe that for adults marijuana is a relatively harmless drug and should be made legal. Others strongly disagree, pointing out that, among other things, continued marijuana use can lead to lung disease. Other side effects include impaired judgment, which makes driving dangerous, elevated heart rate, impaired short-term memory, and, eventually, paranoia and psychosis. Marijuana is thought to be especially dangerous for young people because it interferes with the ability to learn and it can decrease motivation.

Cocaine

Cocaine stimulates the central nervous system, which makes the user feel excited and alert. Cocaine comes in two forms: powder, or small lumps, which is inhaled through the nose or is injected, and crack cocaine, or freebase, which is smoked. Other names for cocaine are coke, snow, flake, nose candy, blow, big C, snowbirds, and white. Crack cocaine is also called rock, french fries, or teeth.

The effects of cocaine are felt quickly, usually in about ten seconds. The user feels up, or high, because the cocaine speeds up the heart rate and blood pressure while narrowing the blood vessels. This combination, however, can produce a seizure, stroke, or heart attack. Using cocaine over time can lead to insomnia, loss of appetite, hallucinations, and paranoia. In addition, cocaine is considered extremely addictive. It causes an intense high, but when the effects wear off, the crash, or depression, is so low that the user will do just about anything to get more to satisfy the craving.

Heroin

In the body, heroin turns into morphine, working in two ways: by depressing the central nervous system and activating pleasure areas of the brain. This combination creates an immediate rush, or high, followed by a feeling of peacefulness. Heroin is highly addictive. The user craves it repeatedly, and attempts to stop usually lead to painful withdrawal.

Other names for heroin are dust, H, horse, smack, junk, shit, scab, black tar, China white, and Mexican mud. An especially powerful blend of heroin began appearing on the streets of U.S. cities in 1994. That August, in New York City alone, it claimed the lives of eight people—the worst case of multiple drug overdose in that city in a decade.

Heroin can be taken in various ways: mainlined, by mixing it with a water solution and in-

Heroin is often mainlined, meaning it is mixed with a water solution and injected into the bloodstream. The drug's powerful sedative effects can be fatal.

jecting it into the bloodstream; popped, injected under the skin; injected into a muscle; sniffed; smoked; or swallowed.

In the short term the user gets drowsy, a state called nodding out. This drowsiness can progress to irregular breathing and heartbeat, cardiac arrest, or coma. Over time heroin use leads to lack of appetite, reduced sex drive, and itching or burning skin. It also produces tolerance, which requires increasing amounts of the drug to maintain the same effect. Another problem is that a person using dirty needles can contract HIV, the virus that causes AIDS, hepatitis, and tetanus.

Hallucinogens

Hallucinogens affect the senses, leading to distorted perceptions of time, space, and mood. Hallucinogens can also produce vivid sights, sounds, colors, tastes, and smells. For some users these distortions are creative and exciting; for others they are terrifying and produce what is known as a bad trip. Depending on the type of hallucinogen, the effects can last from minutes to days, even to weeks. The short- and long-term effects can include panic, confusion, anxiety, and sleeplessness. Some people even have flashbacks, that is, delayed effects even after they stop using the drug. Hallucinogens come in many forms: liquid, powder, pills, gelatin, and, in the case of psilocybin, fresh or dried mushrooms.

Some common hallucinogens are phencyclidine (PCP, angel dust, hog, killer weed, love boat, lovely), lysergic acid diethylamide (LSD, acid, sugar cubes, white lightning, blue heaven, microdot), mescaline and peyote ("mesc," buttons, cactus), and psilocybin (magic mushrooms, "'shrooms").

Designer drugs

The Drug Enforcement Administration (DEA) defines illegal drugs according to their chemical formulas. To get around the law, chemists in underground, or illegal, laboratories are always trying to figure out how to modify the chemical structure of certain drugs. In the mid-1980s the DEA declared designer drugs, also called look-alike or analog drugs, to be controlled substances and therefore subject to legal regulation. Look-alikes get their name from their resemblance to other, genuine drugs. They are not the same, however, because their chemical makeup has been altered. But because new drugs are appearing all the time, it is difficult for the DEA to keep up. Said one DEA official, "Many of the chemicals turn out to be legal—simply because they never existed before, or at least not long enough for someone to pass laws against them."

Designer drugs are made from various combinations of amphetamines, narcotics, and hallucinogens. Depending on the drug, the user might feel agitated, become extremely relaxed, or start hallucinating. Some designer drugs come in the form of pills, others in the form of powders that are inhaled, smoked, or injected. Long-term use can produce symptoms similar to Parkinson's disease, such as drooling, uncontrollable tremors, impaired speech, and brain damage. The psychological effects include depression, anxiety, and paranoia.

Some common designer drugs are analogs of amphetamine (MDMA—also called ecstasy, XTC, Adam, essence—MDM, STP, PMA, 5-DMA, TMA, DOM, DOB, EVE), analog of phencyclidine (PCP, PCPy, PCE), analogs of meperidine (MPTP—also called new heroin—MPPP, synthetic heroin), and analogs of Fentanyl (synthetic heroin, China white).

The rest of the story

These chemical descriptions tell only part of the story. Drugs that are manufactured in underground laboratories are often impure. They have been cut, or diluted with additives. These can include relatively mild substances such as lactose and sucrose, which are two types of sugars, and mannitol, which is used as a mild baby laxative. Other types of additives can be drugs themselves, such as quinine, heroin, or cocaine. Sometimes these additives are toxic—poisonous—or fatal to

Basketball star Len Bias (left) died of a drug overdose in 1986 after smoking an extremely pure form of crack cocaine.

the unsuspecting user. The opposite—that is, a drug that is too pure—can also have disastrous effects. That is probably what killed University of Maryland basketball star Len Bias, who died of a cocaine overdose in 1986, on the eve of his professional career. His friends insisted that this was the first time he had ever used cocaine. Medical examiners say the crack Bias smoked was so pure that it probably caused either a heart attack or stroke.

Another dangerous practice is combining more than one drug, including alcohol. This can multiply the effects—and the risks. Perhaps one of the most famous casualties of mixing drugs was actress Marilyn Monroe, who died of an overdose of alcohol and sleeping pills in 1962. It has never been proved whether her death was accidental or a suicide. More recently, in 1993 actor River Phoenix died from a combination of heroin, marijuana, and morphine.

"People's ability to absorb the drug into their systems—their tolerance—changes from day to day," says Dr. Charles S. Hirsch, the New York City medical examiner. "There is no way of knowing just what a heroin dealer has slipped into the packets he is hustling. It has the potential to kill them every time they use it." Hirsch is speaking about heroin, but his warning applies to many other types of drugs as well.

2

The Causes of Drug Abuse

THERE ARE MANY reasons why people start taking drugs and end up becoming addicted to them. These range from just plain curiosity to the desire to escape life's problems. Whatever the reason, becoming a drug abuser in America is, unfortunately, made easier by the fact that drugs are a widespread part of our culture.

All types of drugs—from aspirin to alcohol—are advertised in the media. The junior high school curriculum for Drug Abuse Resistance Education (D.A.R.E.) contains a whole unit pointing out the ways that people are pressured by advertisers to use drug and alcohol products. These range from snob appeal ("Only rich and famous people use it") to personal testimony ("Drink Macho Beer! Try it, you'll like it!"). Yet there are relatively few antidrug messages to counteract this barrage. In addition, the alcohol and tobacco industries sponsor sporting events, thus linking alcohol and drugs, at least in some people's minds, with the glamorous world of sports. In some communities bars and liquor stores can be found on every block. In still other communities drug deals take place in plain view.

(Opposite page) Women smoke crack in a doorway in downtown Los Angeles. The reasons why people abuse drugs are complex and varied.

29

Even more of an influence is the way drug use is portrayed in popular culture, especially in films and rock music. For over forty years scores of films have played up the fun and glamour of drug use and glossed over the downside. Drugs are portrayed as the playthings of the rich, famous, and fun loving, who seem to use them with relatively mild consequences. In a 1994 film, *Killing Zoe*, a gang of robbers is shown joyriding around the streets of Paris after using heroin and cocaine. In the 1994 film *Pulp Fiction*, the drug dealer's wife mistakenly snorts heroin instead of cocaine; it takes an injection of adrenaline directly into her heart to revive her. Even so, a short time later in the film she is shown sipping a cool drink at an oceanside table—apparently no worse for the incident.

Popular music

Popular music has also contributed to the idea that drugs are fun and trendy, with such songs as the Beatles' "Lucy in the Sky with Diamonds," about LSD, Eric Clapton's "Cocaine," and the Black Crowes' "Sometimes Salvation," complete with a drug-house scene in the video. By the 1990s some bands were even giving themselves drug-related names, such as Jane's Addiction, Cowboy Junkies, and Morphine. Many celebrities have died from drug overdoses, with guitarist Jimi Hendrix and singer Janis Joplin in 1970, comedian John Belushi in 1982, and actor River Phoenix in 1993 among the most notable. But over the years their deaths take on more of a tone of glamour than tragedy. In fact, many have become cult figures.

It is not surprising, then, that many young people conclude that drugs can be part of an exciting and successful lifestyle. They associate being rich, famous, and fun loving with getting high. It

is also not surprising that the triggers for drug use can come from a variety of sources.

Curiosity

Many people first try drugs when they are young, often as an experiment. In many ways this experimentation is understandable. Adolescence is a time of discovering new ideas, trying out new behaviors, making new friends. It is a time of exploring, of taking risks, of testing judgment. Add to this that most young people want to feel grown-up and in control of their lives the way that adults appear to be. Teenagers see their parents and other adults drinking and smoking. In fact, many adults who use alcohol and tobacco do not consider them drugs because they are legal. Young people see attractive models in liquor or cigarette advertisements, and they hear rock musicians singing about the pleasures of getting high. Trying drugs can be one way of feeling older, smarter, and sexier.

Often, "just once" can lead to addiction. That was the case for Mia, an eighteen-year-old who had her first drink at age eleven. Over the next five years she tried a variety of drugs, including marijuana, acid, cocaine, and heroin, until she went through rehabilitation at age sixteen. She says:

> I don't just *think* you can get addicted if you try drugs just once. I *know* you can! Once I tried it, I was hooked. Even though I was basically functioning in my life when I was high—I worked, I was athletic, I went to school. But when you wake up to a pillow full of blood from a bloody nose, you know something is not right!

Mia's addiction began with alcohol, which is not uncommon. In fact, alcohol and tobacco are

called gateway drugs because young people start with them and then turn to marijuana, cocaine, LSD, and other illegal drugs. Alcohol and tobacco, although legal, can become the gateway to addiction.

Physical causes

Many drugs, both legal and illegal, are addictive. That is, people's bodies can get used to them. The drug becomes part of the body's chemical makeup, and eventually the body does not feel well without the drug. This is called building up tolerance. To get the same effect, a person has to take larger and larger amounts of the drug.

Erika, a recovering drug abuser, recalls that she used drugs frequently in the eighth grade; by the ninth grade she was addicted. She cannot remember how often she smoked marijuana:

> All I know is that it started progressing—it was almost out of my control. People say that pot's not addictive, but from my point of view, it definitely is. You get depressed once the high starts to wear off. The more stoned you get, the harder you hit when you come down.

Some researchers believe that drug addiction is a type of disease, that the abuser's body is missing a certain chemical that the drug can supply. Or the body may have too much of a chemical. Either way, the imbalance can lead to psychological problems, such as anxiety or depression.

In addition to physical addiction there can be a psychological addiction as well. Drug users need the rush, or high, to feel good. They worry that they will feel bad if they can no longer have the drug.

The same drug can affect different people differently. For example, the body chemistry of some people is such that even one drink will make them drunk, while others can have many drinks before reaching that stage. Also, research has shown that people who are given narcotics, such as morphine, for medical problems are less likely to become addicted than people who use drugs to escape their problems.

Also, the same drug can affect an individual differently depending on the situation in which the drug is used. These differences are attributed to the influence of what drug counselors call set and setting. *Set* refers to the person's mood before taking the drug; *setting* refers to the situation in which the person took the drug. For example, people who take LSD or smoke marijuana in unpleasant or hostile surroundings are more likely to have a bad trip, or negative experience, than if they were in a pleasant environment.

Dr. Henry Abraham, director of psychiatric research at Saint Elizabeth's Hospital in Boston, has treated many patients with bad LSD reactions over the past twenty years. He believes that certain people are more likely than others to have a severe biological reaction. And there is no predicting when that reaction will occur. For some it happens on the first trip, for others on the 101st. "Taking acid is the equivalent of playing Russian roulette with chemicals," he says.

Personality traits

In general, research has disproved the idea that there is an addictive personality—that is, a set of characteristics that will almost inevitably lead a person to drug addiction. People of every personality type can, and do, become drug users and abusers.

However, there are some types of young people who under certain circumstances are likely to become drug abusers. Some have a particularly difficult time with adolescence. It is a time of physical and emotional changes, some of which

Teenagers puff on a homemade bong at a rally for the legalization of marijuana. Some teens turn to drugs as a way to cope with the difficulties of adolescence.

can be scary. Many teenagers worry a lot: about their appearance, their clothes, their friendships, their futures. For some teens drugs appear to offer an easy way to escape those worries. Drugs can make a nervous person feel calm or a shy person feel outgoing, at least for a while.

Other people are vulnerable to drugs because they have never developed such skills as patience, tolerance, and flexibility necessary for handling life's problems. They typically lack self-esteem and self-control. They have difficulty being assertive and coping with frustration.

Mia puts it this way: "I realized that I did drugs to hide from myself; I was really insecure and had very low self-esteem. But drugs didn't make my insecurities go away. All it did was push them down deeper."

Other types of people who may be at risk for becoming addicted are those who resist authority, are rebellious, and seek thrills and excitement. Dr. Mitchell S. Rosenthal, president of Phoenix House Foundation, America's largest private, nonprofit drug abuse program, says these types of people are drawn to the danger of drugs. "They are seeking adventure, a kind of magic," he says. "They are sort of pharmacologically cliffhanging all the time."

Family relationships and behaviors

Relationships and behaviors within families are another reason that people get involved with drugs. "The earliest and most enduring influence on the child is the family," says the Center for Substance Abuse Prevention (formerly the Office for Substance Abuse Prevention) of the U.S. Department of Health and Human Services. "Being the child of an alcoholic or a drug abuser or having a family history of alcoholism or drug abuse places a child at serious risk of AOD [alcohol and other drug] use."

Researchers disagree, however, about whether this is due more to heredity or environment. Either way, the link between parent and child behavior is strong. Children whose parents use alcohol, tobacco, or other drugs are more likely to begin using drugs themselves and to associate with other youngsters who use. This is especially true if the parents believe that it is all right for people to use alcohol or drugs for having fun or reducing stress.

This link is especially strong if the parents themselves supply alcohol or drugs to their children. Erika is another teenager recovering from drug abuse. Her best friend's mother got the two girls started on wine coolers when they were in the sixth grade. Erika's own parents tried to cover up her drinking and drug problem. One time Erika, high on acid and vodka, threw up all over herself and was sent home from school. She confessed to her father the real reason she was sick. Instead of encouraging her to get professional help, he wrote an excuse to the principal and ignored the problem. Counselors call this covering up enabling.

Other types of families that can put children at risk of using drugs are families where there is conflict and domestic violence, families that are isolated from others in the community, and families that are under stress because of financial, medical, or other problems. Children who are victims of physical, emotional, or sexual abuse—either at the hands of their parents or other adults—are likely to turn to drugs to blot out their pain.

Shannon, thirty-nine, has been straight, or off drugs, for seven years. Shortly after her father sexually abused her in her early teens, she began smoking cigarettes, then marijuana. She soon moved on to LSD, amphetamines, and cocaine. "I was doing anything to stop the feelings," she says.

Children of alcoholics and drug abusers are at an increased risk of abusing drugs.

On a more positive note, children are less likely to become users if their parents do not use alcohol or other drugs, are involved in community or religious activities, and set clear and strict rules about young people's use of substances.

Lack of community support

In addition to individual personality traits and family influences, whether or not people get involved with drugs can also depend on the community they live in. Some communities take a permissive attitude toward drug and alcohol use, even by young people. In these communities, for example, salespeople in convenience stores sell tobacco and alcohol to minors without checking their identification. Judges dismiss drunk drivers or give them light sentences. Teachers and administrators deny that there are drug and alcohol problems in their schools.

In these kinds of neighborhoods problems with drug use are more likely to develop than in neighborhoods where community leaders take strict measures against illegal drug use, especially by young people. This is true whether the neighborhood is rich, middle class, or poor.

"More and more young people are feeling that they do not belong in their communities," says the Center for Substance Abuse Prevention. "They do not identify with their neighbors, they do not feel that people care about their welfare, and they have difficulty finding positive role models."

The center says that these problems can occur in any neighborhood. There are plenty of rich youths whose money and social standing were not enough to save them from the lure of drugs. But people in poor neighborhoods are more at risk because they have fewer resources. There are simply fewer places—such as strong and active

Philadelphia police make arrests after raiding abandoned rowhouses that serve as havens for drug activity. Illegal drug use is especially prevalent in poor, crime-ridden neighborhoods, where citizens often feel a sense of hopelessness.

schools, churches, and community centers— where young people can find positive things to do and good role models.

The sense of hopelessness that sometimes exists in poor neighborhoods also contributes to drug use. Poverty, high rates of crime, especially violent crime, and widespread youth gang activity cause some people to give up on their neighborhoods. These people sometimes use drugs to blot out the misery of their surroundings and their feelings of hopelessness. Some, to support their drug habits, become dealers. They see that dealing can get them big cars, flashy clothes, wads of cash, and the respect of the neighborhood— things they cannot obtain with low-paying jobs.

Peer pressure

Another factor that can lead to drug use is peer pressure. Most young people want to be liked and accepted by their classmates and friends. They want to fit in. So the pressure to do drugs because "everyone is doing it" can be a powerful influence, and research consistently bears this out. For many, saying yes to drugs is a lot easier than saying no. Young people who want to experiment with drugs will find each other. Even young people who were not inclined to try drugs on their own might do so if they associate with friends who have favorable attitudes toward drug use.

This was true for Mia. She recalls, "I thought I was more popular after I started doing drugs because I had a real 'bad attitude'—no fear. It wasn't a good kind of popularity at all, but I got a lot of attention, and at the time I really needed it—even if I had to get it in a negative way."

Desire to stimulate creativity

One final factor in the causes of drug abuse is the desire some people have to stimulate their creativity. For centuries creative people, such as artists, musicians, writers, and scientists, have used drugs to stimulate their talents. The Romantic poets in nineteenth-century England, for example, openly used opium. One of them, Samuel Taylor Coleridge, admitted to taking two grains of the drug before sitting down to write. The late Jim Morrison, lead singer of the rock group the Doors, was usually high when he appeared onstage. His performances were fueled by a variety of substances, including marijuana, LSD, and heroin. Ballet dancer Gelsey Kirkland used amphetamines and cocaine to maintain her slender figure and inspire her dance interpretations.

While using drugs may enhance creativity, the list of creative people who have ruined their careers—not to mention losing their lives—with drugs is a long one, and getting longer. Morrison died of an overdose of heroin at age twenty-seven; Kirkland had to abandon her career when her addiction led to suicidal despair and confinement in a mental hospital.

Musician Charles Neville, one of the Neville Brothers, conquered a longtime heroin addiction. He says:

Using any kind of drugs or chemical substance that alters your physical, psychological, or emotional state is really a trap. The idea that there's something positive to get from it is an illusion. It definitely doesn't help the music. If it hurts the person, it hurts the music.

Today Neville draws his inspiration from the system of exercises called tai chi chuan and the martial arts aikido and jujitsu. "I knew if I wanted to improve or gain anything with my music, then no drugs was the way to go."

A complex picture

As all of this suggests, there is a variety of explanations for why some people use drugs and why some of those people become addicted. Some research indicates that the earlier young people use drugs, the more likely they are to keep using and to increase their use.

Musician Charles Neville, who successfully kicked a longtime heroin addiction, says that the idea that drugs can stimulate creativity is an illusion.

Says Dr. Larry Chait, a researcher on the effects of marijuana and LSD:

Younger children, at eighth-grade level and below, are at greater risk, because their personalities haven't developed well enough, and they aren't mature enough to know how to handle altered states of consciousness. As with any drug, the younger the age of first use, the higher the risk.

There is a lot of evidence that casual use can turn into abuse and addiction unless young people get the support they need from families, friends, teachers, and other adults to channel their curiosity in more positive directions. Someday, researchers may come up with information that will make it much easier to prevent, detect, and treat drug abuse. In the meantime, when trying to understand what causes individuals to abuse drugs, it is important to look at all possibilities, from their physiological makeup to the values of the communities in which they live.

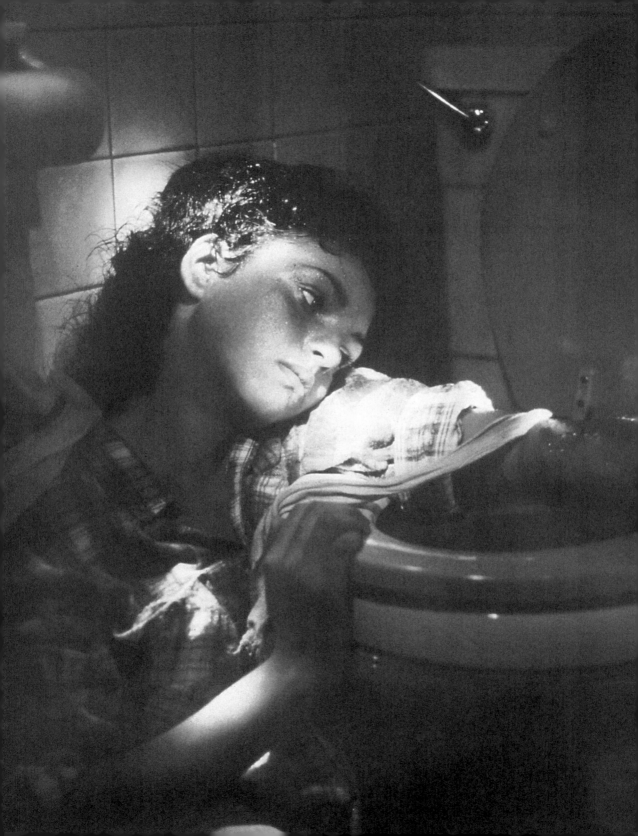

3

The Effects of Drugs on Individuals

DRUGS ARE POWERFUL substances. They can strongly alter people's moods and actions. More importantly, the effects of drug use can have serious short-term and long-term effects—for people's physical and emotional health, for their family and social relationships, and for their ability to learn while in school and to hold down jobs.

Effects on physical health

The physical effects vary with each kind of drug. Regular marijuana use, for example, can cause lung disease, accelerate the heartbeat, and increase blood pressure. It can also interfere with judgment, motor skills, and memory. Cocaine speeds up the heart rate while at the same time constricting the blood vessels. This forces the blood vessels to handle an additional flow of blood, which can lead to a heart attack, seizure, or stroke.

Whatever the drug, regular use can lead to addiction. And once an addiction has formed, if the drug is taken away, the person will develop

(Opposite page) Her arm ravaged by infection from injecting drugs, a young addict shoots up. Drugs are powerful substances that can wreak havoc on a person's physical and emotional health.

43

withdrawal symptoms. These are unpleasant feelings that can range from a mild headache to a full-blown seizure. Other withdrawal symptoms include dizziness, nausea, and nervousness.

Unless withdrawal from a drug is managed carefully, such as in a professionally supervised drug treatment program, users will feel strong cravings to take the drug again. All they can think about is stopping the unpleasant sensations. But taking a drug again after a period of withdrawal leaves a person susceptible to an overdose because the body no longer has any tolerance for the drug.

An overdose can be a serious medical incident. An overdose of heroin, for example, often results in death because it damages the heart and lungs. An overdose of amphetamines, on the other hand, rarely leads to immediate death. But over time amphetamines, especially when injected, can lead to heart problems, lung disease, and diseases of the blood vessels. Hence the common drug culture warning, "speed kills."

Effects on emotional well-being

Some drugs create frightening emotional reactions. LSD, for example, can cause nightmares, panic attacks, continuous visual hallucinations, and even psychosis. When this happens the person becomes mentally unbalanced and loses contact with reality.

Erika, who dropped acid every day during the ninth grade, recalls sometimes seeing LSD trails. This phenomenon occurs when a person sees the image, or trail, of a moving object, such as where a waving hand had just been. Erika says that even eight hours after she took acid, when the other effects would have almost worn off, the scary trails would still be there. At other times she felt unreal. "Once I took acid and felt like I was on another planet," she says. "I didn't know if I was the only person on the earth."

Cocaine brings a different type of emotional reaction. One common result of using too much of the drug is coke bugs, the feeling that invisible insects are crawling all over one's skin. And bugs are not the only imaginary creatures to attack cocaine addicts. Recently a young Florida woman scarred her face for life by clawing at it, trying to pull off imaginary worms.

The anxiety brought on by drugs is very real and very frightening to those experiencing it. One man wrote to syndicated advice columnist Ann Landers about his experience. He had been taking cocaine and crystal meth on and off for several days. He then went into a tanning booth, where he almost passed out. He wrote, "I haven't slept in 57 hours. I believe I may have suffered brain damage. This morning, I tried to recite the ABCs and couldn't do it. I'm scared stiff and can't stop crying."

Accidents

People under the influence of drugs often act foolishly. Their judgment is poor. They take risks that can change their lives forever. Automobile accidents, for example, are the leading cause of death for Americans under the age of twenty-one, according to the National Center for Health Statistics. A large percentage of those accidents happen because a young, inexperienced driver is using alcohol or drugs. Other young people under the influence of drugs feel that they have superhuman powers, such as being able to fly.

One startling example comes from the resort town of Myrtle Beach, South Carolina. In the early summer of 1992, large groups of high school graduates flocked to the town to celebrate. Within just a few days the emergency room at the local hospital reported the following cases: Six teens were treated for alcohol poisoning. Their blood alcohol level ranged from 0.10 percent, which is legal intoxication in most states, to 0.45 percent, which is enough to kill an average person. One sixteen-year-old with a blood alcohol level of 0.18 percent jumped eight feet down a hotel staircase and chipped a vertebra. Another drunken teen, whose blood alcohol level tested at 0.25 percent, died when he leaned over a hotel balcony, fell, and landed on his head.

People under the influence of drugs also lose their inhibitions and put themselves in dangerous situations. One of the most common of these is having unprotected sexual relations. This can lead to contracting a sexually transmitted disease or to an unplanned pregnancy. Mia recalls, "I ended up having sex with guys when I didn't really want to just because I was high. It wasn't exactly against my will; it was just that I was feeling so high that even though I wanted to say 'no,' I just couldn't."

Some addicted women become prostitutes to obtain money to support their drug habit. Brenda, thirty-three, a recovering cocaine addict, describes what happened after she dropped out of a drug rehabilitation program:

A car, mangled from a drunk driving accident, is displayed as a reminder of the dangers of driving while under the influence of alcohol or drugs.

*A drug addict receives fresh
needles from a volunteer for
Prevention Point, a group that
works to curb the spread of
AIDS. Intravenous drug users
who use dirty needles run the
risk of contracting HIV, the
deadly virus that causes AIDS.*

I stayed sober for two weeks after I left, but then I
was back to using cocaine. I started prostituting to
get money. It was terrible. I hated myself. I was
alone, at 2 or 3 in the morning, getting in people's
cars, just thinking about getting high, and afterward feeling so awful. I hated myself.

Eventually Brenda, sick and exhausted, was re-
admitted to the program.

Drugs and AIDS

Another problem for those who inject drugs is
that dirty needles can transmit hepatitis, tetanus,
and the deadly AIDS virus, HIV. AIDS, which is
also spread through sexual contact, is not a disease itself but a set of problems that develop
when the body's immune system shuts down. As
the immune system falters, the body is less and
less able to fend off invading bacteria and viruses.
AIDS can lead to memory loss, pneumonia,
paralysis, blindness, and some types of cancer.
Although scientists have developed drugs that can
slow down the effects of AIDS, they have not yet

figured out a way to restore a person's immune system. Until a cure can be found, a person with AIDS will eventually die from the disease.

Special problems for pregnant women and their babies

The effects of drug abuse are especially damaging for pregnant women and their babies. Even before a baby is conceived, if the woman or man uses drugs, in particular marijuana, it can be difficult for the woman to get pregnant. Drug use during pregnancy places added stress on the woman's body. It can also interfere with healthy habits, such as eating good food and getting enough rest. This can cause such problems as anemia, heart disease, and hepatitis. Also, some drug-addicted women do not get prenatal care, medical care during a pregnancy, because they fear that their drug use will be reported to the authorities.

Using drugs during pregnancy can also result in a difficult birth. Drug use has been linked to breech delivery, in which the baby's buttocks come out first, premature birth, and stillbirth.

Worse, any kind of drug, legal or illegal, will affect the unborn baby, also called a fetus. An estimated 375,000 drug-exposed babies are born each year in the United States. Research is still under way to determine what kinds of drugs, and how much and how often they are taken, will create what kinds of effects. But it is known that in most cases drugs used by the mother will harm the baby. Drug use in the first few months of pregnancy—often before a woman knows that she is pregnant—can damage the baby's organs and tissues. Drug use after the fifth month can interfere with the development of the brain and nervous system.

When a pregnant woman is addicted to drugs, her baby can also become addicted while still inside the womb. As a newborn, the baby then suffers painful withdrawal symptoms, just as an adult going through withdrawal does. Newborns that have been exposed to drugs in utero, or in the mother's womb, experience other problems as well. Those whose mothers smoked marijuana, for example, often have low birth weight, which makes it difficult for them to stay healthy and grow, tremors, and vision problems. Those exposed to narcotics suffer from such disorders as diarrhea, vomiting, sweating, hiccups, rapid breathing, and high-pitched crying.

About 30 percent of women infected with the AIDS virus will pass the virus on to the fetus, according to the Centers for Disease Control and Prevention. That was the case for Mary, a former heroin addict, who has been straight for seven years. But when she was on drugs, she contracted HIV from a dirty needle. Her third child, now age two, was born with AIDS. "I watch my baby getting sicker every day," Mary says. "I wake up every day knowing that I didn't just mess up my life, but that I poisoned my baby. I cry every day for her."

Most babies with AIDS do not live much past childhood. But most drug-exposed babies do. And as these children grow up, they often have disabilities, sometimes for the rest of their lives. These disabilities can by physical, such as breathing and digestive problems, slow reflexes, and poor coordination; mental, such as being slow learners; emotional, such as rarely smiling or laughing; and social, such as having trouble making friends.

Crack babies

Of all the drugs that affect babies in utero, the most damaging is crack cocaine. Crack babies, as they are called, do not go through withdrawal. But the drug cuts off the supply of oxygen to the

A tiny crack baby struggles to stay alive with the aid of a respirator. The babies of mothers who use crack cocaine often suffer long-term effects of the drug, including emotional problems and educational difficulties.

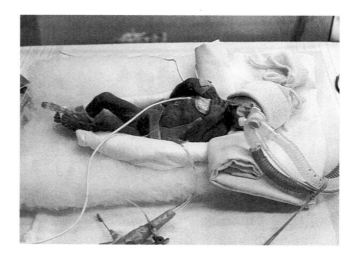

brain, which causes different degrees of brain damage.

When they are newborns and infants, crack babies behave oddly. Unlike most babies, which love to be cuddled, crack babies struggle when someone holds them. They can cry frantically for hours, and no one can comfort them. As they get older, former crack babies are fearful and suspicious of people, and they get frustrated easily. They have trouble in school because they have difficulty concentrating and learning even simple tasks. Since the late 1980s, when crack babies and other children exposed to drugs in utero began entering school in significant numbers, teachers and social workers have worked hard to find ways to meet their serious educational and emotional needs.

Effects on the family and social relationships

Drugs not only harm people physically and emotionally, they can ruin people's relationships with their family and friends as well. Many adult drug abusers end up losing their jobs and families because they care more about getting high than anything else. When they are high, they are sometimes spaced-out, or dazed, and unresponsive; other times they are jumpy and irritable. They argue with family and friends who confront them about their drug use, denying that there is a problem. They can become paranoid; that is, they fear that people are out to get them.

Drug abusers often steal money and property from family and friends to support their habit. Mia stole money from her parents and grandparents. She knew she had reached an all-time low when she sneaked into her grandmother's house and stole some of her jewelry. "I confessed to her, and I really felt ashamed and guilty," Mia says. "I love her so much, and I can't believe that I was so desperate to get high that I would go to the point of ripping her off to buy drugs."

When parents use drugs, they are often emotionally distant from their children and sometimes physically violent. These parents often abandon their responsibility to help their children grow because they are so wrapped up in their own needs. Dorothy, a former drug user, says, "My life was spent getting high. I was up all night. When I was high, I didn't know where my kids were. When I didn't have drugs or alcohol, I was angry at the kids; they were a burden."

Effects on jobs and schooling

Sooner or later most drug abusers lose their jobs. They may be able to hide their addiction for a while. But eventually, because they are more interested in getting high than being productive, their performance on the job deteriorates.

They arrive late and leave early and sometimes skip work altogether. They miss deadlines, make mistakes from not paying attention or using poor judgment, and are generally less efficient. They may even cause injuries to themselves or others because of their carelessness. Despite repeated

Successful Wall Street economist Lawrence Kudlow quit his job and entered a drug rehabilitation program when his drug and alcohol abuse began seriously affecting his job performance. Like Kudlow, most drug abusers eventually find themselves unable to hold down a job.

warnings from their supervisors and coworkers, nothing improves. Except in unusual cases, they eventually get fired.

Even highly paid executives can fall into this trap. Lawrence Kudlow was a successful economist with a top Wall Street investment firm, Bear Stearns. But years of a hectic, high-pressure work life—traveling, writing reports, giving speeches—had led him to abuse cocaine and alcohol. He began losing weight. He canceled meetings or missed them, which irritated colleagues and clients. The final straw came when Kudlow was scheduled to give the keynote speech at a luncheon for two hundred people. He never showed up. Shortly after that Kudlow resigned his position and went into drug rehabilitation.

The effects of drug use are especially destructive for young people, whose main job is learning. The physical effects are harmful for growing bodies. Marijuana, for example, disrupts learning because it impairs short-term memory and comprehension, making it difficult to take in new information. It also interferes with concentration and coordination, making it difficult to learn physical skills, such as driving a car or playing an instrument. Inhalants can cause permanent lung damage. The use of PCP, which blocks pain receptors in the body, can lead to self-inflicted injuries.

In addition, using drugs can interfere with a young person's motivation to undertake meaningful activities, such as study, join after-school activities, or form positive friendships. Drug use can interfere with the skills a young person needs to develop on the way to adulthood, such as the ability to get along with other people. Most importantly, drug use can undermine the development of self-confidence and self-respect, which are critical for meeting life's challenges.

Worth the risk?

Even the casual drug user faces the eventual possibility of deteriorating health, emotional instability, accidents, damaged family and social relationships, and loss of jobs or educational opportunities. Needle-using drug abusers face the risk of contracting HIV, and drug-using women are likely to harm their unborn babies. Most people who begin using drugs do not look ahead to these potential consequences. Yet for the sake of their friends, families, children, neighbors, and coworkers, as well as for their own sake, they might well ask themselves, "Is it worth the risk?"

4

The Drug Trade

IT IS AGAINST THE LAW in the United States to sell illegal drugs or to sell legal drugs illegally. Yet drug sales are booming, and despite intensive efforts by government officials and private citizens' groups, drug trafficking has increased in the last four decades. The term *drug trafficking* covers cultivating, refining, transporting, and selling illegal drugs. Although the drug trade is mostly hidden, or underground, it has had a major impact on the economies of the United States and the world.

The drug sales pyramid

Drug sales of the three major illegal drugs consumed in the United States—heroin, marijuana, and cocaine—can be seen as a pyramid. At the bottom there are teenaged and adult users who sell or sometimes give drugs away to turn on their friends. Above them on the pyramid are small-time street dealers, called pushers, who sell to support their own drug habits. There are also small- and medium-time dealers who do not use drugs themselves but are in business strictly to make money.

At the middle level are criminal organizations that control drug distribution in the United States. Until the mid-1980s most of these organizations

(Opposite page) A Houston police officer displays a huge cache of marijuana seized during a drug bust. Despite intense government efforts to curb the drug trade, illegal drug sales are still booming in the United States.

were part of the Mafia, a criminal organization composed primarily of Italian Americans. More recently, Colombian and Chinese drug importers have taken control of the U.S. distribution networks. These importers rely on youth gangs to distribute the drugs to pushers and dealers. The gangs can be of almost any race or nationality: African American, Hispanic, and white, as well as Colombian and Chinese. It is not uncommon for gang members to be armed with assault rifles and automatic weapons; their beepers keep them alerted to new drug shipments. Gangs use their youngest members—those who are too young to be punished seriously if they are caught—as runners to make drug pickups and deliveries.

At the top of the pyramid of drug sales and distribution around the world are powerful international drug-trafficking organizations, often called cartels. Their leaders are commonly called drug kingpins or drug lords. It is estimated that these drug lords earn $50 to $60 billion in profits every year. For example, Carlos Lehder Rivas, a Colombian drug lord, not only owned his own island in the Bahamas, he built a three-thousand-foot runway there for his planes carrying drug shipments.

Growers, processors, and mules

There are three other groups of people on the drug sales pyramid: growers, processors, and mules. The growers of the three major illegal drugs—cocaine, heroin, and marijuana—are most often poor farmers. They grow drugs because they can make more money than by growing legal crops. In the Chapré Valley of Bolivia, for example, a farmer can earn three times the average income by growing the coca plant, which is turned into cocaine. This crop often makes the difference between crushing poverty and a decent life for the farmer's family.

Colombian drug kingpin Carlos Lehder Rivas bought his own island in the Bahamas with the huge profits of his cocaine-smuggling cartel.

The processors, usually poor peasants, work to turn the raw material into a useable drug. In cocaine production the large, bulky coca leaves must be turned into a paste so that it can be transported more easily. Coca paste is made in what are called coca factories deep in the jungles of Colombia, Bolivia, and Peru. These so-called factories, however, are usually little more than deep pits in which the coca leaves, mixed with chemicals to break them down, are stomped into paste by the processors. The mules, usually gang members, smuggle the paste to an illegal laboratory in another part of the jungle, often far away from the growing area. In the laboratory, usually a structure that can be quickly assembled and taken down, chemists mix still other chemicals with the paste to turn it into powdered cocaine.

Opium goes through a similar, although not as lengthy, process to be turned into heroin. Marijuana production is simple. It needs only to be picked, dried, and crushed to ready it for transport and sale.

The drug lords use terror and violence to make sure their businesses run smoothly and prosper. In

Before being raided by police, this camp in the Bolivian jungle was capable of producing up to 1,500 kilos of cocaine per week. These makeshift jungle laboratories mix coca paste with chemicals to create powdered cocaine.

the past twenty years in Colombia, for example, the drug lords have murdered a dozen supreme court justices, a minister of justice, an antidrug newspaper editor, and scores of police officials. The violence of the drug cartels has also spilled over into other countries. One horrifying case concerned DEA agent Enrique "Kiki" Camarena. In 1985 Camarena headed up an investigation of marijuana plantations in Mexico. One day he disappeared from his office in Mexico City. Several months later his decomposed body was unearthed on the outskirts of the city. He had clearly been tortured and mutilated before being killed.

Drug smuggling

The drug lords smuggle drugs into the United States in various ways and through various ports of entry. For example, every year an estimated three hundred metric tons of cocaine flows into the United States from South America through Central America and into Mexico. It enters the United States mainly through south Florida and the southwestern states of the United States that share the 2,013-mile border with Mexico: Texas, New Mexico, Arizona, and California. The shallow, easy to cross Rio Grande and isolated desert areas on either side of the river make policing very difficult. From there the cocaine funnels through distribution centers in such cities as Los Angeles, Tucson, and Phoenix. When it reaches its destination city, the drug is stored in a safe house for distribution.

There are a variety of methods for importing drugs. Smugglers use planes, trains, and automobiles, including the specially built cigarette boats, so called because of their long, sleek shape. These boats actually go too fast for Coast Guard vessels to catch. Smugglers also hide drugs in luggage, food, animals, and, if necessary, their own bodies. One shipment of heroin even arrived in San Francisco in 1988 by goldfish. Small amounts of the drug, wrapped in cellophane, had been inserted in the bodies of live goldfish.

One common method smugglers use is to swallow small, wrapped packages of drugs. If they are lucky, the packages are excreted in a bowel movement sometime after the smuggler has passed through customs. If they are unlucky, the package breaks open in their digestive systems, which results in overdose and sometimes death.

The trade in heroin, marijuana, and cocaine

Drug trafficking is a complex problem that is difficult to combat in part because each of the major illegal drugs used in the United States today is grown, processed, transported, and distributed in a different way. In addition, those distribution channels are constantly changing in response to pressure from American and international drug officials.

Heroin is made from opium, which is processed from the poppy flower. Until the early 1970s most of the opium was grown in Turkey then refined in laboratories in southern France. When American and international drug enforcement agencies cracked down on these operations, the heroin trade moved to the Golden Triangle. This isolated area is where the borders of Thailand, Laos, and Myanmar, formerly called Burma, meet.

In the late 1970s and 1980s heroin also began coming from the Golden Crescent, remote country areas of Iran, Afghanistan, and Pakistan. Today some opium poppies are also grown in Mexico and Guatemala.

The development of the marijuana trade in the United States has followed a somewhat different course. Until the mid-1970s most of the marijuana sold here was grown abroad, primarily in Mexico,

Marijuana plants found growing in a California forest are hauled off to be destroyed. One-quarter to one-third of the marijuana consumed in the United States is grown domestically.

Jamaica, and Columbia. It is not illegal to grow marijuana in these countries, but their officials usually cooperate with U.S. government efforts to stop drug trafficking. Today most of the imported marijuana, an estimated one thousand metric tons, comes primarily from Jamaica, Mexico, and Colombia.

Marijuana is also grown in the United States, even though this is against the law. Most of it comes from seven states: California, Hawaii, Kansas, Kentucky, Louisiana, Missouri, and Tennessee. This domestic marijuana is cultivated in a variety of locations, ranging from farmland to remote national forests to backyards and window boxes. As law enforcement agencies become more efficient at catching growers, many move their operations indoors to avoid detection. In California, for example, the Drug Enforcement Administration estimates that 19 percent of all marijuana is grown indoors.

Because the growing locations are so diverse and spread out, it is difficult to estimate how much marijuana is grown in the United States today. Many growers raise the crop only for their own use. Nonetheless, officials estimate that U.S. marijuana growers produce about one-quarter to one-third of the total amount of marijuana used in the United States today, or 250 to 300 metric tons.

The development of the cocaine trade in the United States has taken still another course. Until the late 1970s cocaine was an expensive luxury that only well-to-do people could afford to use regularly. The drug lords decided that to increase their profits they should figure out a way to make cocaine affordable for greater numbers of people. So they developed crack cocaine. Crack is cocaine that has been processed into little rocks that can be profitably sold for as little as ten dollars a dose. Highly addictive, the name *crack* comes from the crackling sound it makes when it is smoked. Within a short time in the early 1980s, crack use became widespread, with an estimated eight or nine hundred thousand regular users—serious enough to be called an epidemic.

Today the cocaine and crack trade is controlled by a small group of South Americans who process and export the drug. The most powerful are from the area around Medellín, Colombia's second largest city. Operating from its headquarters in the city, the Medellín cartel directs operations in the rugged jungles of the Andes Mountains. These mountains are filled with secret laboratories, roads, airplane runways, and escape routes used by the drug manufacturers and smugglers.

Drug money

Almost all drug deals are done in cash, which creates a problem for drug dealers. As the money moves up the pyramid, from users to pushers to distributors to kingpins, it grows into huge amounts. However, since this money has been made illegally, it is dirty. That is, it cannot be spent or deposited in banks without arousing suspicion. There is now a law in the United States

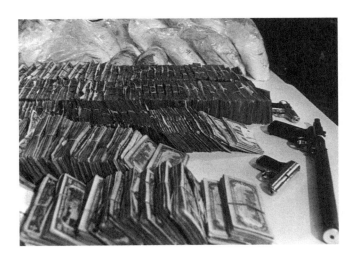

Pictured is millions of dollars' worth of cocaine, weapons, and cash seized by Los Angeles narcotics officers in a series of raids. Cash received in exchange for drugs is called dirty money because it has been made illegally.

requiring that any deposit of ten thousand dollars or more be reported to the Internal Revenue Service, with an explanation of how and where the money was made.

Before this law was passed, however, large amounts of cash flowed into drug-importing areas of the United States. Real estate prices, in particular, escalated out of control. For example, in Miami, Florida, in the 1970s and 1980s it was not uncommon for drug dealers to show up at real estate offices with suitcases full of cash. These cocaine cowboys, as they were nicknamed, bought up lots of expensive waterfront property. This drove up real estate prices and undermined the buying power of local, law-abiding wage earners.

Money laundering

Today the drug lords have become more sophisticated about how they dispose of their cash. Using extensive knowledge of worldwide financial systems, they set up phony corporations and secret bank accounts. This is mostly done through a process called laundering. This means turning dirty money into clean capital that can be deposited in legitimate bank accounts and invested in securities, businesses, or real estate.

It is difficult to estimate how much drug money is laundered each year because the transactions take place underground. But some government officials have estimated the amount at around $300 billion. Some of this money is laundered through U.S. banks. Most of it is laundered overseas through bank accounts set up for fake companies, known as dummy corporations. It is estimated that Panama, for example, has about three hundred thousand such accounts.

Most drug money laundering would not be possible without the help of corrupt, or at least self-interested, banking officials. The corrupt ones take a cut of the profits, between 5 and 10 percent, in return for cooperating with the drug lords. Even bankers who are not getting a direct payment may choose to overlook suspicious transactions because large deposits are profitable for banks. According to one banker in Miami, a point of entry for drugs and hence a city whose banks have a lot of cash reserves, "Many of us didn't ask questions because we didn't really want to hear the answers."

Drugs and crime

Many drug users turn to crime—stealing and even killing—for the money to buy drugs. According to a 1993 study by the Center on Addiction and Substance Abuse at Columbia University, drug abuse is associated with 62 percent of assaults, 52 percent of rapes, 49 percent of murders, and 50 percent of all traffic fatalities and cases of spouse abuse.

Sooner or later most drug abusers who commit crimes get caught. According to the U.S. Department of Justice, approximately 330,000 Americans are in prison for violating drug laws, and there are two to three times that many on probation or parole for the same offenses. About one-fifth of these are first-time or minor offenders, people who are caught with a small amount of a drug or while helping someone carry out a drug transaction.

Many of the other four-fifths are hard-core addicts who will commit almost any crime to support their habit. Criminal justice experts say that seriously addicted heroin users, for example, commit ten times as many thefts, fifteen times as many robberies, and twenty times as many burglaries as offenders who do not use drugs.

Former heroin addict Bill Giddens was an extreme example of this type of addict, but by far not the only one to spread violence and terror in a community. The New York City police described him as a "one-man crime wave." In the two years before he was arrested and sent to prison in 1985, Giddens robbed more than two hundred people. He shot up three or four times a day. To support this ninety-dollar-a-day habit, he attacked people in building entrances or elevators, sometimes committing two or three holdups a day. "His was a life of craving and satiation [satisfaction]," said prison officials. "He knew little of guilt or responsibility."

Gangs and violence

Many poor neighborhoods are dominated by drug-related crime. People often feel unsafe even in their homes and are afraid to walk the streets because gangs control local drug dealings through violence. Many young people in inner-city neighborhoods are forced to join drug-dealing gangs in self-defense. For many, that is their undoing. In a celebrated 1994 Chicago case, eleven-year-old Robert "Yummy" Sandifer was killed by members of his own gang. Sandifer's gang, the Black Disciples, was known to the po-

Police escort members of a drug-dealing gang following their indictment on murder, assault, and narcotics charges. Young people who join such gangs are putting their own and others' lives in jeopardy.

lice for a variety of illegal activities: drug running, car theft, prostitution, and credit card fraud. Sandifer himself had committed an average of one felony a month for the last eighteen months of his life. But life for gang members is always risky. "If you make it to 19 around here, you are a senior citizen," said another Black Disciple. "If you live past that, you're doing real good."

People like Sandifer are killed because of their direct involvement with drugs. Countless other innocent people are killed because they are in the wrong place at the wrong time. They become the accidental victims of drive-by shootings or cases of mistaken identity, or they are easy targets for drug users desperate for money. In Milwaukee, Wisconsin, Norma Deray, seventy-six, was a longtime resident of a neighborhood that had become increasingly rough. One Saturday in January 1995 she took her daily walk to the local grocery store. As she was leaving the store, two young men grabbed her purse—which contained only $4.98—and pushed her down on the icy sidewalk. Two days later Deray died of head injuries.

Health care costs

In all types of communities—poor, working class, and affluent—drug abuse is a drain on public and private health care resources. It drives up health care and related social service costs in many ways. These include treatment for drug overdoses, help for victims of accidents and violence, and extended care for babies who are born addicted.

According to the 1993 report by the Center on Addiction and Substance Abuse, 12 percent of the hospital costs paid by Medicaid nationwide is related to substance abuse, not including tobacco use. This amounts to an estimated $4.4 billion yearly. In addition, substance abusers take longer than other patients to get well when they are hospitalized. Those being treated for pneumonia, burns, and blood poisoning, for example, stay twice as long as people with other types of problems. Finally, thirty-one medical conditions and diseases are linked to drug and alcohol abuse. For example, 51 percent of AIDS cases in children and 36 percent of all hepatitis C cases are attributed to intravenous drug use.

And the problem is spreading

Until the mid-1980s the destructive effects of drug abuse on communities were mostly confined to urban areas. Middle-class whites who wanted to buy drugs usually had to venture into poor, inner-city, mostly minority neighborhoods to buy drugs. More recently, however, drug dealers have expanded their borders. Drug sales have spread into small towns and rural areas. For example, Fort Wayne, Indiana, which calls itself the City of

Churches and has a population of about 173,000, had an estimated seventy crack houses in 1990.

Drug use has also started to rise among students, especially those in wealthy suburbs. According to the annual nationwide drug-use survey conducted by the National Institute on Drug Abuse, in 1990 and 1991—for the first time since 1976—more high school seniors had used LSD than cocaine in the previous twelve months. That same survey found that 14 percent of the high school seniors in Chicago's affluent suburb of Hinsdale had used LSD or some other hallucinogen in the previous year. In some alternative high schools for troubled students in Seattle, Washington, that figure was 90 percent.

In the early 1990s drugs became easier and cheaper to obtain in just about every area of the country and every type of locality. In just one example, in 1994 in Salt Lake City, Utah, marijuana—half of it grown in the state—was plentiful, selling for twenty-five dollars to forty dollars for an eighth of an ounce. LSD, mushrooms, methamphetamine, and cocaine were available in small, affordable amounts at some coffee shops and clubs, with cocaine selling for $20 to $30 for one-quarter of a gram.

Virtually all observers, whatever their perspective about what needs to be done, find these trends alarming. Author Joseph D. Douglass Jr., writing in the January 1992 *Conservative Review,* summarized the views of many experts:

> It would be nice if one could say, as many people seem to be saying, "If they want to fry their brains out, let them." Or, "Do not worry, AIDS will enable the drug problem to solve itself within ten to fifteen years." Or, "Do not worry about the rising number of homicides. It's only the drug dealers killing each other." Unfortunately, it is not that simple. The drug users and drug dealers are taking all of us—and our children—down with them.

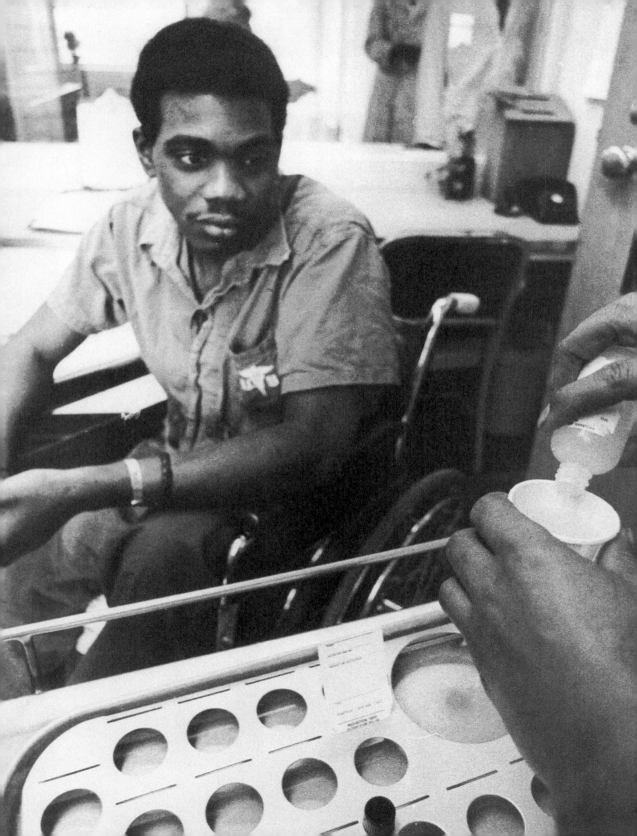

5

Treating Drug Abusers

DESPITE THE FACT that drugs can have a terrible stronghold on people, those addicted to drugs can be helped. Not all drug abusers are able to benefit from treatment, however. Most experts estimate the number of Americans with a serious drug problem at six million. About two million of those are hard-core addicts who do not want to stop using drugs or are so addicted that they cannot stop. Roughly three-quarters of these addicts are hooked on cocaine and one-quarter on heroin; many are also alcoholics or use other types of drugs as well.

That leaves about four million drug abusers who could potentially be rehabilitated. Some of these manage to get off drugs with just the support of family and friends, but most require help from a drug treatment program. Concrete statistics on recovery rates in treatment programs are difficult to pin down because many addicts either do not complete treatment or relapse afterward, sometimes several times over the course of their lives.

Experts are able to estimate recovery rates, however. One estimate comes from Dean Gerstein of the National Opinion Research Center at

(Opposite page) A man undergoing treatment at a hospital drug program receives a dose of methadone, a synthetic drug designed to block the craving for heroin. Like many other drug treatment methods, methadone has had little success in curing addiction.

the University of Chicago. Gerstein, one of the leading experts in the country on treatment effectiveness, has compiled estimates based on his years of research in the field. He has found that about half of the patients entering some kind of treatment program will stay in treatment, and one-half to three-fourths of those will eventually conquer their addictions.

Low success rates

A somewhat gloomier picture is painted by another expert, Joseph A. Califano Jr., a former secretary of the U.S. Department of Health, Education, and Welfare and now president of the Center on Addiction and Substance Abuse at Columbia University. Califano's research indicates that fewer than 25 percent of those who need drug treatment enter a program. Of those, an average of one-quarter complete treatment, and only half of those are drug-free after a year. "In other words," Califano writes in a 1995 *New York Times Sunday Magazine* article, "those entering programs have a one-in-eight chance of being free of drugs a year later. But those odds beat many for long-shot cancer chemotherapies, and research should significantly improve them." Califano also points out that a recent study in California found that even these relatively low success rates are helping to solve the problem of drug addiction. Officials there have found that one dollar invested in treatment saves seven dollars in crime, health care, and welfare costs.

Unfortunately, there are not nearly enough treatment programs nationwide to accommodate all of those who want help with conquering their addictions. The Center on Addiction and Substance Abuse estimates that of the roughly three million addicts who want treatment, only about half—one and a half million people—will get it.

A group of young men takes part in a prison drug treatment program designed to help inmates conquer their addictions. Unfortunately, few federal prisons provide drug treatment services.

Most of the country's approximately five thousand treatment programs have long waiting lists, and some are so crowded they do not even bother to keep waiting lists. In federal prisons, where an estimated 75 to 80 percent of the inmates use drugs, only about 20 percent get help. Crime statistics show that half of these inmates were under the influence of drugs or alcohol when they committed the crimes for which they are serving time. This leads some experts to propose that before being released or paroled, a prisoner should successfully complete a drug treatment program.

Other experts support the concept of treatment on demand for any drug addict. They are urging the federal government to increase funding for treatment programs so that no addict who wants help will be turned away. The 1994 *National Drug Control Strategy*, the official policy statement of the administration of President Bill Clinton, lists as one of its goals to expand treatment capacity and services and to increase treatment effectiveness so that those who need treatment can receive it. "Our goal is treatment on demand," says Lee P. Brown, director of the Office of National Drug Control Policy.

Even if the goal of drug treatment on demand could be achieved, it would still be necessary for policy makers to decide what kinds of treatment are most worthy of funding. Health care professionals, politicians, and even addicts themselves disagree on which types of treatment are the most effective. Over the years hundreds of thousands of dollars have been spent comparing and evaluating different approaches. About the only thing most experts agree on is that the treatment method should be matched to the type of drug the person is addicted to. The individual's personality and home environment should also be taken into account.

Crisis intervention

The first step in recovery is getting a drug abuser into treatment. Most abusers, however, refuse to accept help. They are in denial. That is, they are unwilling to admit that they are addicted. They fool themselves into thinking they can stop using drugs any time they choose. It usually takes a crisis to actually get them to go for help. The crisis can be medical, such as a seizure or heart attack brought on by drug use. It can be legal, such as getting arrested. It can be financial, such as losing a job. Or it can be emotional, such as having a loved one walk out.

Sometimes families, often with the help of health care professionals, come together for what is called an intervention—that is, they confront the abuser and insist that he or she accept help. In some states people can use a legal process called civil commitment to force family members or friends into treatment.

Detoxification

Most drug abusers, when they first come into treatment, need to go through detoxification, nicknamed detox. During this process the body rids itself of all drugs that the abuser has been using. Detox usually takes two or three days, but

some drugs, such as barbiturates, can take a week or more to leave the system. Often during detox medical supervision and treatment are necessary to keep the withdrawal symptoms from becoming too severe.

Treatment services

After going through detox, different treatment, or rehabilitation, options may be offered to the drug abuser. These include residential, or in-patient, treatment; outpatient treatment; a therapeutic community; and a twelve-step program. Despite their differences, these approaches have two elements in common. These are counseling, both individual and group, and support services.

In individual counseling the addict meets one-on-one with a counselor; in group therapy the addicts meet together under the guidance of a trained counselor. This can be a psychiatrist, psychologist, clinical social worker, or other professional trained in alcohol and other drug abuse counseling. The counselor might also be a former addict who has gone through special training.

In both individual and group counseling, the drug abusers are encouraged—sometimes forced—to take an honest look at their drug use. They are required to share private thoughts and

In counseling, drug abusers are encouraged to explore the reasons for their addiction, and to begin making positive changes in their lives.

feelings and to explore the reasons for their addiction. They must admit the problems their drug use has caused for themselves and their loved ones. Sometimes family members are invited to join in these sessions. Most importantly, abusers are encouraged to think about how they can make positive changes in their lives.

Individual and group therapy clearly worked for sixteen-year-old Erika. Before going into treatment, Erika, who had tried just about every drug, became addicted to LSD, dropping, or using, some almost every day. Her family finally committed her to a hospital, where she stayed for two months. She saw a therapist, a counselor, and a psychiatrist daily. Every day she also had three group therapy sessions to attend and at night either an Alcoholics Anonymous (AA) or a Narcotics Anonymous (NA) meeting. All of the meetings took place in the hospital. She recalls the way the hospital conducted its sessions:

> In those daily [group therapy] meetings, you'd have to sit in the middle of the circle. So you'd be in the center of 30 other kids, plus 2 counselors. They'd sit in there and scream at you to make you talk about what you were feeling. It was definitely intimidating. They didn't always take a nice, easy approach. Usually I'd break down and cry. . . . Once I got used to it, though, I realized that everyone else was talking about a lot of the same issues, which made it easier.

Support services

In addition to individual and group counseling, various support services are often used to prepare drug abusers to maintain a drug-free lifestyle when treatment ends. These include job counseling, educational classes, nutritional counseling, and budgeting. Drug abusers with children receive information on how to be better parents. Some recovering abusers may also require ongoing medical treatment to help with their recovery. Cocaine addicts, for example, often receive antidepressant medication to counteract the depression they typically experience in their first year of recovery.

Residential treatment

Drug users who need a structured environment, away from the harmful influences of daily life, may turn to residential treatment. This method is also called inpatient therapy. It lasts anywhere from twenty-eight days to fifteen months. In residential treatment the abuser lives in a controlled, drug-free environment, usually either a hospital or special drug treatment clinic. Each day is highly structured and includes individual and group counseling sessions. As the end of treatment nears, participants receive support services to help make the transition back to their regular lives.

Research indicates that residential programs have the best long-term success rates. The Institute of Medicine, an arm of the National Academy of Sciences, showed in one study that although only 20 to 25 percent of residents remain in residential programs, nearly half of those stayed long enough to benefit from treatment. Their levels of drug use and criminal activity decreased, and their levels of employment increased.

Addicts in residential programs live and receive treatment in a controlled, drug-free environment. These programs have better long-term success rates than outpatient treatment methods.

But residential programs are expensive, anywhere between ten to twenty thousand dollars a year, compared to around three thousand dollars a year for outpatient programs. Well-to-do people and people who work for companies with good health insurance can afford these fees. People with moderate incomes and poor people obviously cannot, and there are a limited number of openings in public, nonprofit treatment centers.

Therapeutic communities

A variation of residential treatment is the therapeutic community. As in other residential treatment programs, participants in therapeutic communities live on the premises. However, therapeutic communities differ from regular residential programs in two major respects: they are often run by former drug abusers who have received special training, and they use the technique of confrontation. The largest of these programs today is Phoenix House, founded in New York City in 1967 by five recovering heroin addicts. It operates fourteen centers on the East and West Coasts. Sixty percent of their staff members are former drug abusers.

With the confrontation technique, the group leaders and members are tough on abusers, prodding them until they admit their drug use. The goal is to resocialize them. This means retraining them so that they will be more honest, take responsibility for their actions, and care about the effect they have on other people. Residents are responsible for doing the housekeeping and cooking. Therapeutic communities are stressful places and dropout rates are high—around 50 to 60 percent. And the process of treatment is long, usually taking a minimum of eighteen months. The biggest criticism of therapeutic communities is that they brainwash their members. But these programs are often the last hope of drug abusers who have dropped out of other programs.

Halfway houses

Making the transition from a residential program or therapeutic community to a normal life can be tough. Halfway houses help with that transition. They provide a place to live while the drug abuser gets used to living a drug-free life. Most halfway houses offer treatment services as well, but the daily routine is less structured than in a full residential program.

Mary, a fifty-one-year-old executive secretary, recalls:

> I feared the idea of a halfway house. I had the image of a dirty, rat-infested place of black drug addicts and lesbians. But once I was there I found it didn't matter what our backgrounds were. We were all sick. There was a camaraderie [fellowship] for each other that really helped. It didn't matter what the stories were, of drugs or sex, or what color we were. None of us had a decent life.

Outpatient treatment

Some drug abusers can benefit from living at home and going to work, school, or job training while working on overcoming a drug problem. For these people, outpatient treatment may offer the best option. Outpatient programs allow users to visit the hospital or clinic several times a week for individual and group counseling and for support services. They are also encouraged to attend support groups such as Alcoholics Anonymous or Narcotics Anonymous.

The advantage of outpatient treatment is that it is the least disruptive to the abuser's life and family. Outpatient programs are also less expensive than residential programs, an average of three thousand dollars a year versus ten to twenty thousand dollars. The disadvantage is that the abuser is still in the environment that led to the addiction. Outpatient treatment works best with abusers who are strongly committed to getting off drugs. It is also helpful if they are able to change their home and neighborhood environments to ones that support a drug-free lifestyle.

Twelve-step programs

Some drug abusers are able to recover solely through a twelve-step program. Others use a twelve-step program in combination with formal treatment programs or for maintaining sobriety after formal treatment ends. The twelve-step method, developed by Alcoholics Anonymous, has proved successful in rehabilitating alcoholics since the mid-1930s. The approach has been adapted by such groups as Narcotics Anonymous and Cocaine Anonymous to help rehabilitate drug abusers. Twelve-step programs use the principle of self-help. That is, group members, all of whom have the same problem, give each other support and understanding. No professional counselors are involved, and there is no charge for services. Drug abusers systematically work through twelve steps to overcome their problem. They admit their

A speaker talks to members at an Alcoholics Anonymous meeting. This program uses the twelve-step approach to overcoming addiction, which is based on the principle of self-help.

problem to other group members and pledge to fight their addiction one day at a time. They never consider themselves recover*ed,* only recover*ing,* because they will never be free of the temptation to abuse drugs and so must make a daily commitment not to use them.

Success rates for twelve-step programs are difficult to obtain because, in order to protect their members' anonymity, the programs discourage intrusions by researchers and other outsiders. But the few studies that have been done suggest similar or slightly better recovery rates than for treatment programs. That is, somewhere between 25 to 30 percent of group members stay clean and sober for up to five years. The major criticism of twelve-step programs is that they do not require members to stop using drugs in order to participate. Members who come to a meeting high, for example, can disrupt the recovery work of other members. Another criticism is that the emphasis on God, which some members call their higher power, is too religious for some addicts.

Methadone maintenance

Another drug treatment method that has been in use since the 1960s is methadone maintenance. Methadone is a synthetic drug that blocks the craving for heroin. It is distributed to heroin addicts through medically supervised clinics. When methadone was first developed as an alternative to heroin, it was cheered as a miracle. The hope was that addicts would gradually become weaned from methadone and learn to lead productive lives. Best of all, it was thought, crime associated with heroin use would drop dramatically since addicts would not need to steal and murder to support their habit.

Unfortunately, that hope was not realized. Today many addicts are not only hooked on

A man is congratulated after successfully completing a drug rehabilitation program. As is true for all recovering addicts, remaining drug-free will be a difficult, lifelong commitment.

methadone, but they are hooked on other drugs as well. Most methadone clinics do not have the funds to provide the counseling services that would help addicts change their lives. And methadone is now sold illegally, just as other drugs are.

And then what?

Successfully completing treatment is just the first step in recovering from drug abuse. The hard work has just begun. It can take up to four months of intensive outpatient treatment for in-patient treatment to be successful. And it can take years of commitment to a drug-free life for a former addict to lose the constant fear of relapsing.

The first step after treatment, leaving the sheltered environment of residential treatment or a halfway house, can be especially difficult. Erika recalls her feelings about leaving her rehabilitation, or rehab, program: "When it came time to leave, I didn't want to. I was scared, and I cried a lot. The first few days at home were really difficult, especially having to deal with my parents again."

Even then, the average recovering drug addict experiences five relapses on the road to recovery. The craving for drugs can be triggered by any number of things, such as running into a drug-using friend or dreaming about getting high. In the early months of her recovery, Mia had what she calls a major slip. She had stopped going to AA meetings and began spending time with people who got drunk. Drinking started to look appealing to her, and she convinced herself that it would be all right to drink but not use drugs.

At a party she started drinking beer. "The next day, it felt like it was a bad dream," she recalls. "I went straight to my dealer's house and bought a gram of coke. From there, it was acid to mushrooms to pills to smoking rocks. I know my next step would have been shooting up if I hadn't gone back to AA."

Professionals and recovering addicts agree that it takes many years of hard work to overcome a drug addiction and lead a clean life. The support of family, friends, and—for some—twelve-step groups is essential during shaky periods.

As Erika says:

> Sometimes I still want to go back to the hospital because I felt safe there. No one was going to hurt me—most importantly, myself. Out here, I could hurt myself by starting to use again. But my whole family got involved in my recovery. If I ever go out and there's alcohol around and I'm uncomfortable, I'll call one of my parents to come and pick me up.

In addition to the controversies about which types of treatment work best, there are also controversies about how to best allocate the limited drug treatment funds available. Some experts believe it would be better to put resources into the less expensive outpatient programs. Others say that money should be spent on special programs for adolescents, who may have the best chance for long-term success. Still others argue that while residential programs may be expensive, they are less expensive than other related costs that are currently draining the economy. Drug Strategies, a nonprofit, public policy organization in Washington, D.C., estimates that it costs between $30,000 and $40,000 to keep a drug addict in prison for a year. Medical treatment for an intravenous (IV) drug user who has contracted AIDS can cost over $100,000 a year.

While health care professionals are debating the best ways to stop people's demand for drugs, law enforcement officials are debating the best way to stop the supply of drugs.

6

The War on Drugs

THE FEDERAL GOVERNMENT, often working in cooperation with state and local authorities, has tried a variety of ways to deal with America's drug problem. The first major effort began in 1969, when President Richard Nixon named drugs as a major threat to the health and welfare of all Americans and called for government action. Every president since then has addressed the drug problem in different ways, but always through some combination of law enforcement, treatment, and drug prevention education.

In the 1980s President Ronald Reagan emphasized law enforcement over treatment. His administration was also concerned with preventing casual drug use by middle-class people. First Lady Nancy Reagan toured the country with her "Just Say No" campaign, which emphasized willpower and high morals. The goal of the campaign was to persuade people, especially young people, to stop using drugs or never to start. President George Bush, who first used the term "war on drugs" in a 1989 speech, also concentrated his antidrug efforts on law enforcement. About 70 percent of Bush's budget went for law enforcement. The other 30 percent went for treatment

(Opposite page) While the problem of drugs in the United States often seems insurmountable, it is one that must be tackled. These young antidrug marchers in Detroit remain hopeful that the war on drugs can be won.

Nancy Reagan greets young members of the local "Just Say No" club. The First Lady toured the country, encouraging young people to "just say no" to drugs and alcohol.

and prevention. The major push of the war on drugs was to cut down on the supply of illegal drugs. Bush aimed to close off U.S. borders to prevent drugs from being smuggled in, an approach called border interdiction, and to pressure drug-producing countries to stop producing and distributing drugs. He called for harsher penalties for dealers and users.

Bush administration officials used a variety of tactics to reach these goals. They set up agencies such as the Counter-Narcotics Center within the Central Intelligence Agency and the Financial Crimes Enforcement Network to combat money laundering. They installed surveillance balloons along the border with Mexico and increased border patrol forces. U.S. Navy, Air Force, Coast Guard, and Customs Service personnel searched the seas looking for drug shipments.

In South America DEA agents and American and other military units conducted extensive searches in Colombia, Bolivia, and Peru for drug kingpins and their laboratories. The U.S. government gave funds to political leaders in those countries to be used for fighting drug traffickers and to encourage growers to switch to crops other than coca leaves.

Harsher punishments

Back at home, government officials concentrated on rounding up dealers and users. State and local governments were pressured to enact tougher punishments for recreational and casual drug users. These included suspending drivers' licenses, canceling government benefits such as college loans, and requiring civil fines of up to ten thousand dollars for possession of even small amounts of most controlled substances. In an effort to reduce the number of drug-addicted babies being born, pregnant women who used drugs began to be prosecuted for exposing their unborn babies to drugs. Many companies began programs for drug testing in the workplace to screen out drug users. These were coupled with employee assistance programs, which provide confidential counseling and referral for employees who need help.

In 1984 Congress enacted the Comprehensive Crime Control Act. One of its key provisions was to establish mandatory minimum sentences for the illegal possession or sale of any type of drug, no matter what the amount. Some typical sentences were five years in prison for possession of a gram of LSD or five grams of cocaine. Additional antidrug legislation in 1986, 1988, and 1990 made these penalties even stiffer. Forty-nine states also enacted their own mandatory minimum sentencing laws.

The Bush administration also addressed treatment. In his first year in office, for example, he

Agents display hundreds of pounds of cocaine seized during a U.S. Customs and National Guard operation. Despite such efforts, the illegal drug supply in the United States remains plentiful.

A speedboat seized by U.S. Customs officials during a drug raid. The war on drugs has resulted in the seizure of millions of dollars' worth of property from drug dealers.

increased funding for treatment programs by about 50 percent, to $1.6 billion. Most of this money was sent to states in the form of grants. The states in turn distributed the funds to clinics and therapeutic communities for treatment and to other organizations for public-education campaigns.

Successes

All of these efforts paid off—to a limited extent. Several South American countries signed agreements with the United States to cooperate with American antidrug programs. Others passed tough laws to fight money laundering. U.S. officials seized millions of dollars' worth of property from drug dealers: cash, cars, planes, real estate, and ships, as well as drugs.

In just one example, in April 1990 the Federal Bureau of Investigation went public with its two-year undercover operation, Cat-com, for the term "catch communications." Informers had been planted inside drug gangs and gathered information through electronic eavesdropping. Cat-com helped break up the U.S. operations of seven Colombian drug rings and led to the arrest of sixty-eight people. Other operations in 1989 and 1990 resulted in the arrest and extradition, or being sent to another country for trial, of such drug kingpins as Carlos Lehder Rivas and Panamanian dictator Manuel Noriega.

Perhaps most significant is that casual drug use in the United States did, in fact, decline. Federal surveys indicated that what they defined as occasional drug use—within the past year but less often than monthly—decreased from 5.8 million users in 1988 to 3.4 million users in 1992, a 41 percent decline. This decline occurred primarily among middle-class Americans. They reported reasons such as problems with health, finances, work, or pressure from a spouse or lover.

The war on drugs is far from over

Despite these successes, however, most experts today say that two decades of concentrated effort have made little impact. "The great drug triumph of the Reagan-Bush years—the decline in the number of marijuana and cocaine users—produced few visible social benefits," says drug enforcement authority Mark A. R. Kleiman, an associate professor of public policy at the John F. Kennedy School of Government at Harvard University. "Hard-core problem users were not the ones who stopped using drugs. But they are where the crime, violence and disorder come from."

Critics of past government policies cite a number of reasons for the basic failure of previous government efforts to reduce drug use in the United States. Cutting off the supply of drugs has

GAMBLE ©1989 THE FLORIDA TIMES-UNION: KING FEATURES SYNDICATE

proved to be nearly impossible. Although the top leaders in several South American countries pledged to work with U.S. antidrug efforts, corruption at lower levels of government undermined these agreements. Drug crops are so abundant that crop-eradication efforts did not work. And for every South American cocaine laboratory that was raided and shut down, a new one popped up.

Border interdiction has not been successful, either. Guarding seventy-five hundred miles of U.S. borders with Mexico and Canada and three hundred ports of entry has proved unmanageable for U.S. officials. Their efforts have simply forced drug traffickers to come up with new supply routes and more sophisticated smuggling techniques. And although many drug lords were arrested and sent to prison, others have taken their place.

Although there are more DEA officials stationed around the world than ever before, the production of drugs has reached new levels. Federal law enforcement authorities say that cocaine imports have not decreased and that heroin imports have actually increased. Other drugs, such as LSD and designer drugs, are available in greater supply and purity than ever before.

Perhaps the most serious effects of the war on drugs have occurred in the criminal justice system. U.S. jails and prisons are filled to overflowing. As of June 1994, according to the Bureau of Justice Statistics, for the first time in U.S. history more than one million people were behind bars. There were 919,143 in state prisons and 93,708 in federal prisons, more than double the number who were in prison at the end of 1984.

Much of this increase is the result of drug arrests. According to the bureau, in the last ten years the number of arrests for drug-law violations has doubled, and those arrested are five times more likely to go to prison. Criminal justice experts attribute this increase to the strict laws

DEA agents take suspected marijuana smugglers into custody. The number of arrests for drug-law violations has doubled in the past ten years.

and regulations put in place during the Reagan and Bush administrations.

Problems persist

In 1994 President Bill Clinton declared that previous drug-control strategies had worked to only a limited extent. The 1994 *National Drug Control Strategy* executive summary reports that the federal government has spent $52 billion on drug-related efforts since 1988. The report states:

> While [these efforts have] achieved some success, illegal drugs continue to pose a significant threat to the country. Hardcore drug use continues unabated, drug-related crime and violence have not dropped significantly, and recent studies indicate that our young are returning to drug use.

Many experts are calling for a shift in federal drug policy from a law enforcement approach to one that emphasizes treatment and prevention. In 1993 and 1994, for example, publications as diverse as the *Journal of the American Medical Association, Police News, Rolling Stone*, and the *National Review* all carried articles on the need to change federal, state, and local policies.

"We need to stop filling our prisons with petty dealers and unlucky users and focus our criminal-justice resources on those who commit violent and predatory crimes," wrote Ethan Nadelmann, an assistant professor at Princeton University's Woodrow Wilson School of Public and International Affairs, in the May 5, 1994, issue of *Rolling Stone*. "And we need to stop believing that abstinence is the sole solution to drug use."

Even officials who support stiff penalties for other types of crimes are beginning to realize that mandatory minimum sentencing policies are not working. Republican George Pataki was elected governor of New York State in the fall of 1994 on a tough anticrime platform. But by early 1995 he was calling for easing up on harsh sentences for drug offenders in favor of drug rehabilitation, job training, and community service. As Lee P. Brown, director of the Office of National Control Policy, said in early 1995, "I've been a cop for over 30 years, and I've arrested many drug users. I know we can't arrest ourselves out of this problem."

Shift in focus

The 1994 *National Drug Control Strategy* proposes to shift the focus of government efforts back toward treatment and prevention. It moves the focus away from casual drug use and places it on the harder to reach part of the drug-using population: hard-core users. It also promises that the United States will continue to help countries that want to stop drug use and drug trafficking.

The federal government's 1995 antidrug budget, as outlined in the 1994 *National Drug Control Strategy*, calls for $13.2 billion, most of which will go toward treatment programs targeted at hard-core drug abusers. These programs will

A police officer speaks about the dangers of drug use. The federal government is increasing time and money spent on drug prevention and treatment programs.

emphasize treatment services for special populations, such as adults and adolescents under the supervision of the criminal justice system; pregnant women; and women with dependent children.

The strategy also calls for shifting funds away from border interdiction and placing them in programs to fight drug production abroad. Special help will be given to countries that have demonstrated their willingness to cooperate with the United States to stop drug trafficking.

There is also money in the budget for U.S. communities that want to fight drugs at the local level. Some of the special programs to be funded are school-based programs that provide prevention and education services for children and families at risk for substance abuse, peer-based programs that teach young people how to resist peer pressure to use drugs, and family-based programs that help family members develop better skills for communicating and resolving their conflicts.

Other experts on drugs feel that the federal government's programs will still not solve the problem. One view is that treating drug abuse as a crime has as much chance of working as Prohibition did. Prohibition, the period in the United States from 1920 to 1933 when it was forbidden to manufacture, transport, sell, or possess any alcoholic beverages, was enacted to reduce the crime and violence associated with drinking. It did not work, however. Ordinary people broke the law in order to drink, and organized crime took over the illegal manufacture of alcohol, called bootlegging.

Drug legalization

Prohibition's failure prompts some experts to propose removing criminal penalties for, or decriminalizing, possession and selling of small amounts of marijuana. The money now spent on

law enforcement could be spent on treatment and prevention. Advocates of this solution point out that in the 1970s eleven states decriminalized marijuana without a major increase in marijuana use.

Some advocates support making other drugs, such as cocaine, legal as well. They say that although this move might increase drug use somewhat, it would dramatically reduce the crime and violence associated with the underground, or black market, sale and distribution of drugs that are now illegal. Just as with alcohol, certain drugs would be taxed and their distribution regulated. "Legalizing drugs would put the big dealers and their gun-toting distributors out of business," wrote *New York Times* columnist Max Frankel in December 1994. "It would also keep most users from having to steal to support the habit. That alone would liberate a great deal of money and energy for reclaiming wrecked lives and neighborhoods."

Others disagree strongly with the idea of legalizing any drugs, saying that the idea would backfire. The number of addicts would increase dramatically, as would crime. The most harmful effects would be felt in America's central cities. James A. Inciardi and Duane C. McBride, authors of *The Drug Legalization Debate*, write, "The social fabric of the ghetto is already tattered, and drugs are further shredding what is left of the fragile ghetto family. . . . The legalization of drugs . . . would serve to legitimate the chemical destruction of an urban generation and culture." They point out that since 1986 in New York City crack use has led to a 225 percent increase in cases of child abuse and neglect related to drugs. There has also been a dramatic increase in the numbers of drug-addicted newborns, infants abandoned in city hospitals, and children neglected, beaten, or killed by drug-addicted parents.

Many communities throughout the United States realize that they cannot depend on federal or state governments to help solve their drug problem. In some communities, individuals and small groups are tackling the drug problem them-

Missouri students and teachers march in solidarity against drugs. Fed up with drug use and drug-related crime in their neighborhoods, many communities are taking action.

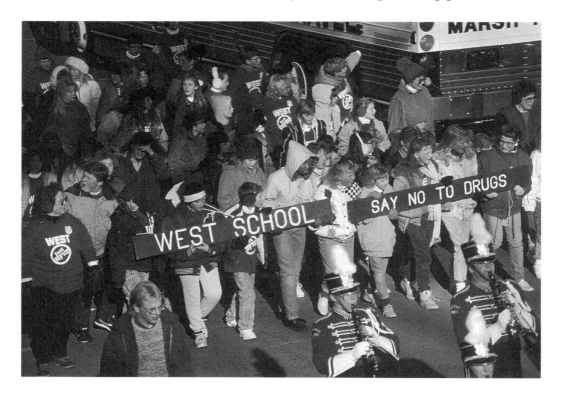

selves. Some of these efforts began in response to a community tragedy, such as a young person's overdosing or dying in a drug-related accident. In Englewood, Colorado, for example, Tom and Jan Kay began giving presentations in the schools on the dangers of using inhalants after their fifteen-year-old son, Brad, died in 1992 of heart failure after huffing butane.

Community efforts

In many localities different groups are cooperating to figure out what will work best in their community. These groups include the schools, parents, civic groups, religious organizations, police and courts, social services, health care organizations, business and industry, and the media. These community actions take different forms. Some neighborhood groups hold antidrug marches and rallies. Others patrol known drug-dealing areas, looking for drug houses and drug dealers. They write down license plate numbers and descriptions of the dealers and report them to the police. Anonymous drug-reporting hotlines are another widespread tactic. Some neighborhood groups even risk confronting drug dealers directly.

Many antidrug activists pressure elected officials to clear drug dealers off the streets. One strategy is to tear down or renovate drug houses, abandoned buildings that are used for drug transactions. Another is to create safe havens for youth who are not yet using drugs or who want to stop. In Santa Cruz, California, for example, the Fenix Project targeted a poor neighborhood where drug sales occurred on the streets and gangs ruled the alleys. The project brought together young people, local park service employees, and the community at large. They cleaned up and renovated a park so that young people would have a safe gathering spot.

A Maryland police officer teaches the D.A.R.E. curriculum to a class of fifth-graders. The D.A.R.E. program has proved effective at reducing drug use among students.

Other efforts focus on educational programs, especially those aimed at improving the self-esteem and coping skills of young people. In New Orleans, Louisiana, the Alcohol and Drug Abuse Community Prevention Project of the New Orleans public schools offered free after-school programming for African American children. In addition to play activities, project staff supervised homework exercises and led self-esteem building groups. Students who participated in the program showed significant improvement on standardized tests.

Drug prevention programs

Another strategy is to stress prevention. Drug-prevention groups publish informational pamphlets and sponsor antidrug talks and other activities. Some volunteers staff hotlines to answer people's questions about drug and alcohol use. Schools, health care programs, and social service agencies provide counseling for young people with drug problems. Local television and radio stations and newspapers carry public-service programming about drug prevention.

One of the best known of these prevention programs is D.A.R.E. (Drug Abuse Resistance Education), which has reached millions of schoolchildren since its founding in 1983 in Los Angeles. D.A.R.E. uses uniformed police officers as classroom instructors who deliver a seventeen-part curriculum to elementary and middle-school students. Evaluations of D.A.R.E. in the Los Angeles schools indicated that students who receive the D.A.R.E. curriculum in elementary school show greater improvement during their first semester in junior high compared with non-D.A.R.E. students. Seventh-grade students who had received D.A.R.E. in the sixth grade indicated significantly lower drug use than students who had not participated in the program.

Lee P. Brown, director of the Office of National Drug Control Policy, applauds all of these efforts. In the preface to the 1994 *National Drug Control Strategy*, he wrote a message to all Americans:

> Drugs are not a problem solely of the poor, of minorities, or of inner-city residents. . . . The problem is neither liberal nor conservative, Republican nor Democrat. . . . It affects all Americans. . . . Your leadership is critical to the success of our mutual efforts to reduce drug abuse and drug-related violence.

Appendix

Saying No and Other Ways to
Fight Back Against Drugs

Ways to say no
- Just say "no thanks" and walk away.
- Give an excuse or a reason, such as "I don't like how it makes me feel."
- Change the subject.
- Avoid places where people use drugs.
- Just ignore the person or group.

Fighting back
- Make friends with people who do not use drugs.
- Join a program like D.A.R.E. (Drug Abuse Resistance Education) or ask an adult to help you start a "Just Say No" club.
- Get high without drugs, such as through sports and hobbies.

If your friend has a drug problem
- Learn more about drug abuse and treatment, such as by reading this and other books on the subject.
- Find out where in town your friend can get help, such as by looking in the yellow pages under "Drug Abuse."
- Ask a school counselor, teacher, or clergyperson about where to get help. You do not have to give your friend's name.
- Tell your friend, in words that are right for you, how it makes you feel when your friend gets high. Suggest that your friend get help. Do not try to talk when your friend is high.
- Remember that you cannot change the mind of a friend who does not want help. You can only explain how much you care.

Glossary

addiction: The inability to stop using a drug. An addiction can be physical or psychological.

cartel: An organization of businesspeople that makes decisions about the price and marketing of a product.

coca: The large, treelike plant from which cocaine is made.

dependence: Relying on a drug, such as to get through the day or to enjoy oneself at a party.

detoxification, detox: The process of ridding the body of a drug.

drug: A chemical that acts on the brain and nervous system; it can cause changes in feelings, behavior, and the way the body functions.

drug trafficking: The cultivation, sale, and distribution of illegal drugs.

enabling: Allowing a person's drug habit to continue by helping to cover it up.

flashback: A delayed effect of a drug that occurs after a person has stopped using the drug.

hallucination: An illusion of seeing, hearing, or otherwise sensing something that does not exist.

harm reduction: An approach to drug abuse prevention that tries to reduce the harm that drug addicts do to themselves and society.

interdiction, border interdiction: Guarding the U.S. borders to prevent drugs from being smuggled in.

intoxication: The state of being high, either excited or sluggish, on alcohol or drugs.

intravenous, IV: Injecting drugs into the veins.

laundering: The process of changing the cash received from drug deals into untraceable, "clean" money that can be banked and declared on tax returns.

overdose: Taking more of a drug than the body can handle.

pharmacology: The properties and reactions of drugs.

pusher: A drug dealer.

recovery: The process of getting off and staying off of alcohol or drugs.

rehabilitation, rehab: A program or process that helps a drug user return to sobriety and health.

safe house: A location where illegal drugs are stored.

tolerance: The process by which a drug becomes part of the body's chemical makeup. Eventually the body does not feel well without the drug, and increasing amounts must be taken to get the same effect.

withdrawal: The painful physical and psychological symptoms that result when an addicted person stops using a drug.

Organizations to Contact

The following organizations have information about drug abuse and its effects. Some also can provide referrals for where to get help. The addresses and phone numbers are included to help you obtain more information directly from the organizations. To find local treatment centers for drug addiction, try the yellow pages under "Drug Abuse and Addiction Information." In the white pages check for your local Alcoholics Anonymous, Cocaine Anonymous, Narcotics Anonymous, and council on alcohol and drug abuse.

Cocaine Helpline
(800) COCAINE

This is a round-the-clock information and referral service. Recovering cocaine-addict counselors answer the telephones, offer guidance, and refer drug users and family members to local public and private treatment centers.

D.A.R.E. America
Box 2090
Los Angeles, CA 90051-0090
(800) 223-DARE

The Drug Abuse Resistance Education (D.A.R.E.) program was created in 1983 by the Los Angeles Police Department and the Los Angeles Unified School District. Specially trained police officers visit fifth- and sixth-grade classrooms weekly for seventeen weeks to teach students how to refuse drugs and alcohol. D.A.R.E. also conducts programs for kindergarten through fourth-grade students and for students in junior and senior high schools.

Drug Policy Foundation
4455 Connecticut Ave. NW, Suite B-500
Washington, DC 20008-2302
(202) 537-5005

This foundation is comprised of scholars, policy makers, and concerned citizens working for responsible reform of current U.S. drug policies. It offers a variety of publications, including books, newsletters, and position papers. The foundation supports the legalization of some drugs and increasing the number of treatment programs for addicts.

Hazelden Foundation
Pleasant Valley Rd. Box 176
Center City, MN 55012-0176
(800) 328-9000

This private foundation distributes educational materials and self-help literature for participants in twelve-step recovery programs and for professionals who work in the field of substance-abuse prevention and treatment.

The Heritage Foundation
214 Massachusetts Ave. NE
Washington, DC 20002
(202) 546-4400

This foundation is a conservative public policy research institute. It opposes the legalization of drugs and supports increasing law enforcement efforts to stop drug abuse. It offers a variety of publications, including newsletters, position papers, and books.

"Just Say No" International
2101 Webster St., Suite 1300
Oakland, CA 94612
(800) 258-2766
in California: (510) 451-6666

This organization organizes clubs that provide support and positive peer reinforcement to young people. It offers workshops and seminars, publishes newsletters, and conducts a variety of other activities aimed at preventing drug use.

Narcotics Anonymous (NA)
P.O. Box 9999
Van Nuys, CA 91409
(818) 780-3951

This program, founded on the twelve-step principles first developed by Alcoholics Anonymous, is a fellowship of men and women who meet to help one another with their drug dependency problems.

National Clearinghouse for Alcohol and Drug Information (NCADI)
P.O. Box 2345
Rockville, MD 20847-2345
(800) SAY-NO-TO (DRUGS)

NCADI is a resource for alcohol and other drug information. It carries a wide variety of publications, videotapes, and computer-disk-based products dealing with alcohol and other drug abuse.

National Council on Alcoholism and Drug Dependence Hopeline (NCADD)
(800) 622-2255

This national hotline provides information and referrals for people seeking counseling for a drug or alcohol problem. Callers are given the telephone number of the NCADD affiliate nearest them; they can also choose to receive written information on dependence.

Phoenix House Foundation
164 W. 74th St.
New York, NY 10023
(212) 595-5810

Phoenix House was founded in 1967 by recovering heroin addicts. Today it is the largest private substance-abuse treatment program in the United States, with fourteen centers across the country. It opposes the legalization of drugs and works to focus federal drug policy on the needs of hard-core drug abusers.

Suggestions for Further Reading

David Bender and Bruno Leone, eds., *Drug Abuse.* Opposing Viewpoints Series. San Diego: Greenhaven Press, 1994.

Phil Brashler, "Taking It to the Streets," *Chicago Tribune Sunday Magazine*, September 4, 1994.

Drug Abuse Resistance Education (D.A.R.E.) Instructional Guide for the Junior High. Los Angeles: Los Angeles Unified School District, 1984.

Jonathan Harris, *Drugged America.* New York: Four Winds Press, 1991.

Margaret O. Hyde, *Know About Drugs*, 3rd ed. New York: Walker and Company, 1990.

Office for Substance Abuse Prevention, *What You Can Do About Drug Use in America.* Washington, DC: U.S. Department of Health and Human Services, 1990.

Rolling Stone, "Drugs in America: The Phony War, the Real Crisis" (special issue), May 5, 1994.

Gail B. Stewart, *Drug Trafficking.* San Diego: Lucent Books, 1990.

Barry Stimmel, *The Facts About Drug Use.* Washington, DC: Drug Policy Foundation, 1991.

Mike Tidwell, *In the Shadow of the White House.* Washington, DC: Drug Policy Foundation, 1993.

Additional Works Consulted

Joseph A. Califano Jr., "It's Drugs, Stupid," *The New York Times Sunday Magazine*, January 29, 1995.

Center for Substance Abuse Prevention, *Signs of Effectiveness in Preventing Alcohol and Other Drug Problems*. Washington, DC: U.S. Department of Health and Human Services, 1993.

The Drug Policy Foundation, *Choose Health, Not War: Drug Policy in Transition*. Washington, DC: Drug Policy Foundation, January 14, 1993.

Max Frankel, "O.K., Call It War," *The New York Times Sunday Magazine*, December 18, 1994.

Journal of the American Medical Association, "Drug Prohibition—Time to Reconsider?" (special issue), June 1, 1994.

Michael Massing, "Whatever Happened to the 'War on Drugs'?" *The New York Times Book Review*, June 11, 1992.

Monitoring the Future Study. Ann Arbor, MI: Institute for Social Research, University of Michigan (news release and summary), January 31, 1994.

Office for Substance Abuse Prevention, *Drug-Free Communities: Turning Awareness into Action*. Rockville, MD: U.S. Department of Health and Human Services, 1989.

Office of National Drug Control Policy, *National Drug Control Strategy* (executive summary). Washington, DC: The White House, Office of the President, April 1994.

Public Health Service, *National Household Survey on Drug Abuse, Population Estimates 1992*. Washington, DC: U.S. Department of Health and Human Services, October 1993.

Soft Is the Heart of a Child (conference summary). Milwaukee, WI: Milwaukee Council on Alcoholism and Drug Dependence, October 1993.

U.S. Department of Education, *Growing Up Free: A Parent's Guide to Prevention*. Washington, DC: U.S. Department of Education, 1989.

Index

About the Author

Carolyn Kott Washburne received a bachelor's degree in English literature from Wellesley College and a master of social work from the University of Pennsylvania.

After fifteen years as a social worker, she became a full-time freelance writer. Her magazine articles have appeared in *The New York Times*, the *Chicago Tribune, Mademoiselle, Ms.*, and the *Utne Reader*. She is the author of two books for adults and four books for children. She also teaches writing at the University of Wisconsin-Milwaukee.

Carolyn, who has a grown daughter, Jessie, lives in Milwaukee with her son, Charles.

Picture Credits

Cover photo: © Michael Krasowitz/FPG International
AP/Wide World Photos, 6, 9, 10, 15, 39, 41, 52, 56, 57, 64, 68, 78, 93
© Donna Binder/Impact Visuals, 80
© Eddie Birch/Unicorn Stock Photos, 42
© Bill Burke/Impact Visuals, 96
© David Cummings/ Unicorn Stock Photos, 46
© Larry Downing/Woodfin Camp & Associates, Inc., 86
© Jeff Greenberg/Unicorn Stock Photos, 73
© Charles Gupton/Uniphoto Picture Agency, 37
© Ansell Horn/Impact Visuals, 50
© A. Katz/Impact Visuals, 35
© D & I MacDonald/Unicorn Stock Photos, 23
© Dennis MacDonald/Unicorn Stock Photos, 12, 91
© Mike Morris/Unicorn Stock Photos, 94
© Steve Payne/Uniphoto Picture Agency, 74
© Alon Reininger/Unicorn Stock Photos, 8, 28, 60
Reuters/Bettmann, 47, 61
UPI/Bettmann, 17, 19, 21, 26, 54, 75, 84, 85, 89
© Jim West/Impact Visuals, 82
© Charlyn Zlotnik/Woodfin Camp & Associates, Inc., 71